jivaka

the child who healed

jivaka

the child who healed

MALAVIKA KAPUR

Vitasta

Let Knowledge Spread

Published by
Renu Kaul Verma
Vitasta Publishing Pvt Ltd
2/15, Ansari Road, Daryaganj
New Delhi - 110 002
info@vitastapublishing.com

ISBN 978-93-82711-11-7

Cover Design & Layout by Vitasta Publishing Pvt Ltd
Illustration on the cover is by K K Hebbar
Printed by Vikas Computer and Printers, New Delhi

Prof N C Surya, my teacher, living
proof that one can change one's self
completely if one chooses to
and
Surya Narayana Karanth, my cousin, a
man who gave everything to the world
and owed nothing

Acknowledgements

I am grateful to the ashrams and sanyasis at the foothills of the Himalayas; all the friends who had read the manuscript and sought clarifications; Prof Gilles Bibeau for reading the manuscript and appreciating it. My heartfelt thanks to all the old and new friends who read the story and kept me going: Lalitha, Sheela, Prabha, Dorothy and Rajalakshmi. I also thank Renu and Vitasta for being interested in this kind of novel; and the Hebbar Art Foundation for permission to reproduce the cover page line drawing by K K Hebbar.

Preface

The novel attempts at bringing to life child care in ancient India—built around *Kashyapa Samhita*, an ancient text, the only text of Ayurvedic paediatric medicine in existence today.

Kashyapa Samhita has an alternate title, the *Vridda Jivakiya Tantra*—unusual as none of the other *Samhitas* are named after their scribes. Jivaka, the scribe of the tome, was a child prodigy. The novel emerges out of a powerful image of ancient scholars testing the child by forcing him to submerge himself in the River Ganga to prove his merit. He succeeds, emerging as an ancient old healer.

The first part in its eight chapters describes the fictional child prodigy Jivaka growing up (between 5th and 12th century

AD). The second part describes yet another Jivaka, possibly a descendent of the first Jivaka, the scribe of *Kashyapa Samhita*. These five chapters give a glimpse of a modern day-prodigy. The third part continues with the story of the ancient Jivaka growing up.

The story is set on the banks of Ganga, with the mystique of the Ganga and the Himalayas woven into the fabric of the story. The story alternates between the two time frames, past and present, and two children who are both prodigies. The story juxtaposes the modern day Jivaka who is training to be a modern day paediatrician, with the ancient. The novel moves seamlessly in time, focusing on healing practices embedded in spirituality that are still relevant today. The memories and dreams provide continuity to the narrative.

The story is enlivened by the author's experiences as a child psychologist and an avid trekker in awe of the mighty Himalayas and the Ganga.

The Past

Becoming The Ganga

Vatsayani sat brooding by the side of Gangamayya, with her feet feeling the chill of the water. She was daydreaming. One day she would marry a scholar like her father. She would participate in lengthy discussions on the *Upanishads*. She would come to love her scholar husband and have a baby. He would be someone special…very special. "Hey, Vatsa, come, come, what are you doing there?" Her four younger sisters were washing clothes, rubbing soap nuts hard to produce the froth. "We will tell Maa you did not help! Just because you are going to be a bride, don't think you can get away from daily work. Come, come…."

Vatsayani's said, "Who says I am going to be a bride? I am going to marry a scholar." She sighed dramatically, walked towards her sisters. Radha, Chaya and Kathyayini, fourteen, eleven and nine years, all stopped giggling. Five-year-old Munni said, "Ha! Ha, tell me, is Didi getting married? When? When?"

Radha whispered. "I overheard father and mother talking last night!"

Vatsayani sat down and pulled her braid down.

"What were they saying?"

"I am not quite sure—it was more like they were arguing."

"Tell me! Tell me!"

> "Mother says: Vatsa is 15 now, if we don't get her married before she matures, we are in trouble—what about the other four girls?"
>
> "Father says indifferently: She is only a child yet. I will find a good boy for her."
>
> "Mother says: You sit there the whole time with dreams in your head and books in your hands. You have spoilt her thoroughly by teaching her to read, write and even allowing her to sit in and talk in public when other scholars come for discussion."
>
> "Father says: But she wants to learn. Look at the other girls, they are like you—with no interest in anything."
>
> "Mother says: But they are good-tempered, they help me all the time around the house and with the baby too."

"Father says: You get them married—I will get Vatsa married—when someone suitable comes."

"Mother says: Stop being silly."

Mother never spoke harshly or rudely ever to the father.

"What do you mean—Someone will come looking for her? Who are you? The King? We are poor Brahmins. You may be a Pandit but you have no money. Day-to-day living is hard enough. I have put up with your dreaminess for twentyseven years. Now it is time I put my foot down. In case you have forgotten, we have five daughters and only one little boy. By the time he grows up to take over responsibilities, we may not even be there. We need to get the girls married. All the girls of Vatsa's age are already married and have children. All you do is sit there, eyes closed to the reality. Now you have to listen to me!"

Vatsa whispered, "What did father say?"

Radha said, "I peeped and saw. He sat with head lowered and did not say anything for a while!"

After a long time he simply said, 'You are right, my dear, you are right. I feel that they are all still the babies I held in my hands!'

Mother stroked his cheeks and said gently, 'We live in a hard and real world. May I have your permission to proceed with what needs to be done?' He sighed and said, 'Yes.'

Radha added, "He did not want to agree, but he saw that

she was right!"

"What do you mean? She is right?" Vatsa raised her voice. "Why should they get us married just because others are married? Are we cattle? I want to learn more. Get to know the ways of the world!"

Radha said softly, "Didi—there is more!"

Vatsayani sat up, "What?"

> Mother says, "I have found someone in the next village, a young widower who is willing to marry our daughter for nothing—no dowry. I have saved the gold I brought when I came to this home as a bride. I made it into five portions and will give it to each of the girls."

Vatsa said, "But Mother won't have anything left."

Radha said, "Yes, but for her, it is important that we get married!"

> Father is not bothered about the gold. He says, "Widower? How old? Educated?"
>
> Mother sighes, "He is in his thirties, with a fifteen-year-old son. No, he is not a scholar. He works on his land!"
>
> Father says, "He is an old man. He is almost my age. What are you talking about?"
>
> Mother says, "He has agreed—a simple wedding—no expenses for us. He needs a woman for the house."
>
> Father says, "My Vatsa?"
>
> Mother says, "Yes—your Vatsa. Be practical."

The girls were quiet. Only the sounds of the Ganga flowing filled the air! The youngest, Munni said, "Didi is marrying an old man?"

Radha said, "Shut up." Looked at Vatsayani's face and instantly understands the horror to befall her.

Vatsa, for once, was silent. She was the oldest. She was the sacrificial lamb. She had to agree.

Radha said, "Our father was persuaded and he agreed with great reluctance." Radha then hugged Vatsayani, with tears in her eyes, "I am sorry Didi—I am sorry—I did not know that you would not like it. For me and the girls in the village, it would seem a good proposition. Of course, you are different. You have always been different—a koel in the nest of crows! But we love you. We want you to be happy. Go ahead and refuse, we are with you."

Vatsayani said, "I know you all love me. So does my mother. For your sake I must accept. But part of me refuses to accept the second best. Radha, I don't know what to do! I simply don't know, I cannot even ask our father. He has already given up the fight."

Radha, "One more thing. Why the desperation? You know you are a 'mangalika'. Your horoscope is not good for the husband. That's why the unspoken haste."

Vatsayani, "That is a load of rubbish—a superstition." Radha pointed out, "But most people, including the prospective families of bridegrooms, believe in it."

Vatsayani said, "Do I have no say in the matter?" The girls

came and hugged her tearfully. Vatsayani was dry-eyed.

She took a dip in the Ganga and prayed, "Gangamayya, please do something—anything to save me." And then walked home with her sisters.

When mother broached the subject later in the day, both she and father expected fireworks from their volatile daughter. There were none. They were pleasantly surprised but felt uneasy.

A week later, the wedding day dawned. After bathing in the Ganga, Vatsayani was dressed up and mother put a four-strand long gold necklace around her neck. The *muhurtam* —the auspicious moment was at *godhuli*—dusk, when the cows come home raising dust in their wake.

Vatsayani did not say a word.

At noon, she suddenly knew that her world had changed! She knew about it, all of them knew when mother sat outside, every month for three days, when she and her sisters had to do all the household chores. She went quietly to her mother and said, "Maa! It has happened to me, what you have every month." Mother almost collapsed with shock. She screamed, "Oh, ill-fated girl! Could it not have waited for another day! What am I to do?" She started crying. She was not one to cry easily and openly.

Father came and found the girls huddled in a corner. Mother weeping, Vatsayani standing alone, stone-faced in a corner. Father took one look.

Vatsayani said, "It is not my fault."

He said, "Okay. I will go to their house and explain the situation. He is an older person. He will understand. It is not that there are thousands of guests or anything. We will have the wedding anytime after three days on an auspicious day. I will check on that." He went away.

Mother was angry with Vatsayani, the girls, the baby, the whole world. Radha set up a corner for Vatsayani to sit in, and kept a vessel of drinking water. Vatsayani was in her wedding finery. Nothing fancy—a saree of silk and her mother's four-strand gold necklace. Radha quietly brought her food in a plate and kept it near her. Vatsayani knew the routine. She seethed with rage inside. Had this not happened, she would have been married to an old man she did not honour or love. Maybe the Ganga did something for her. Gave her the chance to escape. Vatsayani was almost on fire. She could not sleep and sat up, staring ahead. Radha kept coming to her whispering, "Didi, go to sleep. Things will get better soon." Vatsayani did not reply. Her thoughts span out of control. Who was her mother to decide her fate? What gave her the right? Who was her father? A coward who could not protect his daughter against the conventions of a village full of superstitious morons. What use all his scholarship if he could not do the right thing for his daughter? Radha and her sisters were young and did not know what was good for them. She would go away. No matter where. She would go. If worse came to the worst, she would ask Gangamayya to take her. It could not be worse than marrying a person with a son of her own age!

After raging anger against the family and the whole world, Vatsayani started thinking calmly. "It is my life. I can take it in my own hand. I owe my family nothing. If I am removed from the scene with my managika horoscope, my sisters will have a smooth sailing. If the family does not know where I am and believe me to be dead, they will mourn but eventually get over it. But if I marry that man whom I already detest, I will have a very long and very unhappy life till I die. So it is worth taking a risk for loving a scholar and having his baby."

It was almost two hours past midnight. The sisters were asleep, huddled together as puppies on a winter night. Only Munni had moved away in sleep—probably searching for Vatsayani on whom she usually flung her arms or legs as she slept. "I am going to miss my Munni." Of course, Krishna, the precious one, slept with his parents. Vatsayani's jealousy was stoked at the injustice of it. "I will have a son. A son who will be me!" She vowed. She softly spoke to Munni, woke her up and said, "Munni, I am going to Gangamayya. I am not coming back." Munni mumbled, "Okay, Didi" and turned her back and slept. Vatsayani smiled fondly, tearfully, kissed her forehead and left in her bridal finery, covered with a coarse black blanket given to her for the night. She prayed to Gangamayya from a distance and said, "I will bathe in you when I am pure. Please guide me—show me the path!" She decided to move up the river. If they looked for her, they would go down the river to find her body.

At four in the morning, near the tiny temple on the banks of the Ganga in the thickly wooded mountainous region, she heard the bells and chants of Ganga worship. After the morning prayers, she saw the priest walking away to the village. She could not enter the temple at that point of time as she was menstruating. She sat under a tree and wondered how to survive, a single girl in the wilderness. She could not go to the villages. As a Brahmin girl without a chaperone she would be hounded by rogues and ruffians. She would rest during the day and walk during the night. She had heard from the scholars that there were ashrams in Kanakhala that gave shelter to the needy. She was definitely needy. It might take ten-twenty days. If she were caught, she would be married to this man, who was so desperate that he would even marry a runaway girl!

Fear lent her wings through the bridle paths in the forest, in the northerly direction. Following the Dhruva star—of course, she knew that stars and planets were different. How could these silly people believe in astrology when astronomy was such an evolved science? "Mangalika, indeed," she spat out!

She would go to the river to bathe and pray to Gangamayya at four in the morning. Sometimes she would find in the temple along the way fruit and cooked prasad. She would generously help herself. She was no longer Vatsayani. She was the daughter of the Ganga. She was also the Ganga. Once someone saves you, you are their child and become part of them. The Ganga saved her. It is the Ganga's duty to protect her and give her the scholar's child! She smiled to herself. Too much daydreaming was the bane of her life.

The days were getting hotter. She had lost count. At night, walking through the forest was scary. Due to the Ganga's blessing, already the moon was waxing, lighting her path. Yet she tripped constantly over roots and rocks, stubbing toes and twisting ankles. The shrubs all looked alike, thorny or not. She had to roll the blanket and carry it, as the nights too were hot. Mosquitoes and thorns created a criss-cross of bloody streaks on arms and legs. Thanks to the Ganga, the rains were yet to start. At least there were no leeches. She hoped she could reach Kanakhala before the rains.

She would, in the night, be startled by a cheetah or a sambhar deer. They were all right. But she had to quietly hide if she sensed the elephants grazing. Once she heard the stamping feet and alarm calls of the spotted deer and hooting of the langurs, she knew that the predators were around. She folded her blanket, kept it under a tree and climbed up and sat there, shivering with fear and not cold.

It was a night of the full moon. She saw the tiger moving along the bridle path where she had walked a few minutes earlier before taking shelter in a tree. Thank the Ganga, it did not even look up. It simply walked towards the river. Apparently it had already fed and was thirsty. She stayed there till next day, when all the sounds of the forests returned to normal. No alarm calls, no hoots of the langurs. For the first time in days, she walked to the Ganga in the middle of the day. She bathed, prayed and thanked the river. She was sure people did not come around when they heard a prowling tiger with its occasional growls and roars.

But she must move on. God knew how far she had to go. She was full of bruises and cuts. She felt weak and dizzy. She had found nothing to eat for almost three days. She found she was not able to walk even in the middle of the day. She said, "Gangamayya—if this is the time for me to depart from this world—please let me know. I want to die in your lap." The last thought was that she was sleeping peacefully on Gangamayya's lap.

Doors To Shiva at Kanakhala

Kanakhala, a place that several centuries later came to be known as Haridwar, holiest of holy of the Hindu cities, was tiny compared to what it is today. Old man Ramananda, with his bent back was looking for root vegetables. Suddenly he came across this waif, a young girl with long dark hair, wrapped in a blanket on the path. "My God, what is this? Is she dead? Is she murdered? Oh! My, oh my...," mumbling, he came near. She appeared to be sleeping. He said "Hey girl, wake up—you scared me—you gave a heart attack to an old man!" She did not respond. He sprinkled water from his kamandal. She still did not respond. "Oh my! Oh my! What will I do? I am an old man. There is no one around. I cannot leave her here and go for help. I have to take her." He unwrapped his blanket placed her on it and started dragging it. He muttered, "I hope there are no big stones or thorns that may hurt her. But I have no option. If she does not like it—it is her problem—actually her fault!" he muttered.

By the time he reached the ashram, dragging his burden, he was drenched in perspiration, breathing hard. He sat down, in the shade outside the simple hut. He said to himself, "What am I going to tell Richika? I have brought a girl into the ashram. He is a nice fellow. But a girl in a *brahmachari's* ashram? Scandalous! Why did I not leave her where I found her and minded my own business? I really don't know what he will say. But then again, how can I leave the girl to die alone in a forest? At least, I can give her decent cremation and allow her to merge with Gangamayya and go to heaven. She would have been taken by beasts if I had left her."

He checked on her and found her still unconscious. He put his hands on her forehead. Raging fever! Poor thing! He sighed.

Richika was sitting poring over his books. Ramananda sat quietly till he looked up and said, "What?" Ramananda said, "I was in the forest gathering wild berries and roots...and then..." He stopped. Richika: "That's what you normally do... so what is new?" He smiled. Ramananda said, "I found...I found..." "What? What did you find?" Ramananda said, "I am an old fool. Please don't get angry with me." Richika was alarmed. He said, "When have I been angry with you? You are the father

I never had. You can do no wrong Tata!" Seeing that the old man was indeed distraught, Richika closed the book, got up and came to him, hugged him. "Tata! Tata! Don't worry...Tell me what is it that you are so upset about?" Ramananda said, "You would be angry, but I take the entire responsibility." He could not contain himself. "I found an unconscious girl in the forest. I could not leave her there to die. I brought her here!"

"A girl here? How did you manage it? You are so frail yourself."

Ramananda smiled. "Just like you to worry about me rather than what I did! I dragged her in a blanket!" Richika said, "That's all right then. Take care of her. Ask Sage Kashyapa about what to do about her unconsciousness. When she recovers, send her home or take her to her home. See! No big deal!"

Ramananda was amazed. No wonder he had to take care of Richika. He was a brilliant scholar, but bit soft in the head when it came to common sense. Anyway, showing her to Sage Kashyapa was good advice. He was thinking of her cremation, of all things. That is what old brains do. Think of cremation!

Ramananda asked Richika. "Don't you want to see her?" "If you want me to I will. Where is she?"

"Outside under the shade of the holy peepal tree."

When Richika saw the bedraggled, wounded fair waif, still unconscious, his heart sank. He turned away. He said gruffly, "Tata, please see to it that she is treated and sent home!"

Ramananda smiled. "Thank you. I will do that. She will not be a bother to you in any way."

Richika went back to his books. The old man walked to Sage Kashyapa's ashram. Kashyapa said, "I treat only children." The old man said, "It is only a girl child. Come, please come. You know how helpless Richika is." Being compassionate, Sage Kashyapa came. He took one look. "She has not eaten for days. She has been starving. I will give some ointments for her bruises and cuts. You give her lots of water, thin milk and start giving weak gruel. She will be all right. No, she is not dying. Right now give her some whey or barley water with salt and jaggery. I will give you a little silver spouted cup that we use for feeding the babies. Once she gets something in her stomach, she will recover."

Kashyapa was right. She was a hardy little thing. She was up and about in no time. She made herself useful around the ashram. Getting up at four in the morning, cleaning not only Richika's ashram grounds but also of Sage Kashyapa. She hung around the old man calling him 'Tata'. Generally talking a lot but not a word about who she was and where she came from except her name. That, she said, was Ganga.

Weeks passed. Ramananda was nowhere near sending her home. For Richika, it was as if she was not around. He never seemed even to notice that the ashram grounds were tidy, all the dry leaves swept off. The food cooked just so and it tasted so good. Ramananda was healthier and enjoyed the pampering by this waif. But this could not be a permanent arrangement. Richika was bound to notice her. Especially since she had this habit of listening behind the doors when scholars came to discuss matters of importance with Richika.

Once he asked her, "Where did you learn to read and write?"

She said, "In my previous birth before I became Ganga." Laughingly, she added, "As a man of advanced age and wisdom, don't you know the saying: Never ask the origins of the River, the Rishi and a Woman." Ramananda could not believe his ears. He said, "What are you? Pandita Gargi?" She simply said, "I am just Ganga. You are my father. You gave me life. I am forever beholden to you." Then Ramananda had nothing to say. Sometimes, he even wondered if she was really Ganga in human form. He tried to find some faults in her. Frailties she had none. He was worried. He worried about her future.

Then a strange thing happened. The scholars had come for discussion. One of them stridently said, "No, Gayathri or Savithri is a hymn that is denied to women. It is sacred and out of bounds to women." From her usual hiding place, Ganga replied, "That is totally a wrong interpretation. Prayers to the Sun God are not the prerogative of men. Sun shines equally on men, women, beasts and earth. Praying is our fundamental right. It is like saying woman cannot pray to mother Ganga."

Ramananda was shocked and infuriated at her impudence. But of course, as always, she was bold. She had jeopardised her life for the matter of principle. Stupid girl! He walked in and was obsequious to the scholars. "Please forgive me. It is my granddaughter from the village visiting me. Please forgive me." The stunned scholar who wanted to deny the right of women to recite Gayathri mantra said, "Where did she learn to speak in Sanskrit like that?" The old man said, "My son must have taught this impudent chit of a girl! Please forgive us," and whisked her away to the riverbank.

He started raving and ranting. "What am I to do with you? Now you have to go. We cannot have you stay here as everyone will come to know. Till now only Sage Kashyapa knew, as you were so kindly cleaning the yard of his ashram. Forget Richika. He may not even notice that you spoke!"

Ganga looked him in the eyes and said, "I love Richika. I wanted to be noticed by him!"

Ramananda said, "This is scandalous. I treat you like a child and you—you shameless woman—you think like a prostitute! I cannot believe this of you. You say you are Ganga. What kind of talk is this? I am ashamed of you."

"Tata, I am sorry I have upset you. But it is true. I have never loved anyone before. I have fallen in love with Richika... in these short few weeks. He has done nothing to make me feel like this. I love his face. I love his looks. I love the way he walks and speaks. I have never seen anyone like him. I love his gentleness. My mind is constantly filled with thoughts about him."

Ramananda knew that this stupid girl was sincere. Of course, it was also natural. "Look, this cannot go on. You have to leave this place."

"Why can't he marry me?"

"He is a rishi. That's why."

"There is no such rule. Many rishis marry and have wives."

"How would you persuade him to break his vow of celibacy and marry you? Don't be foolish. Go away before I am blamed for keeping you in the ashram. Go to another ashram, where there are women sanyasinis who will talk sense into you. Go to Tehri. You will find shelter. Please Ganga, please, I beg that you go away before further damage is done. I beg you with folded hands!"

Ganga had tears in her eyes. "Please, Tata, don't say things like this. You are right. I will go away. I am the cursed one. I bring misery to those who shelter me. Give me one more day I will go—I promise I will go!" Placing trust in her words, Ramananda went to rest.

It was twelve days since her last period. If she had to fulfill her life's ambition, this was the time. She would never get a chance again. She went to the Ganga and had a bath. Prayed to the Ganga for what she wanted, keeping Richika's glorious body and brilliant mind in her thoughts. She wanted to go to the little temple after collecting a fistful of rice and some ghee in the Bhoj leaves. She saw Ramananda, bowed down and said, "I will go to the temple to offer my prayers before I leave tomorrow."

The old man felt bad but his loyalty was to Richika. Not to this brazen chit of a girl. He was sure that she was quite capable of taking care of herself.

He shook his head to clear the unkind thoughts. He smiled.

He said, "I bless you my child, may you get what you deserve."

Ganga was joyous that a Brahmin, a holy man, had blessed her. She went to the temple and offered burning oblation to Lord Vishnu. When she came out of the temple, the sun was setting. She worshipped the sun with Savithri prayers. As the sun went down, the moon rose across the Ganga, above the low mountains. The mountains that stood on the other side of the Ganga, those she always thought as elephants with stringy dark hair. She prayed to the moon. With a single prayer she worshipped them all. "May I have a son from Richika and may he be like Richika in his body and mind."

As she returned to the ashram, she was at peace. She knew that what she had so desperately wished for would happen.

Richika was strangely restless at night as he lay on his wooden pallet. He could not read as usual. The girl's argument with the scholars had not annoyed him. It had enlightened him. Normally she was like a mouse. One hardly noticed her. The moon beams passing through the wooden bars of the window lit up the wall into a black tapestry. Suddenly he heard a swishing sound. The door opened—he saw a vision. A goddess walked in with an oil wick lamp in her hands. She had her hair loose, reaching her hips. She had on a silken saree and a gold necklace with four strands. She was an ethereal beauty. A ghost! His hair stood on ends. His whole body trembled with strange tremors. Then he came down to earth. It was no ghost. It was the girl—the waif who had looked like a drowned rat a few weeks ago. She had certainly turned out to be a beauty. Her face was aglow with the golden light of the lamp.

He said, “What are you doing here? I did not mind your question today. You were right and he was wrong. Now you can go. Ramananda must have sent you to apologise.”

She said, “I know I have nothing to apologise for. But I came for something else.”

Richika was curious. “What?”

She said, “I love you—I want your son!”

He said, “What?”

She calmly repeated, “I love you, you are like a psychological tattoo all over me. Painful but true. I love you. All I want is a son from you!”

Richika said, “You are young—you don't know what you are saying. You are impressionable. I am a celibate scholar. I have taken a vow of celibacy. I know no woman. I keep my heart pure.”

She asked, “How would women make you impure? How can the love of a woman make you impure?”

Richika had no answer.

“I know nothing about sex!”

“Nor do I! But we can learn from each other!”

“I am a rishi. I cannot have a wife or family.”

“You know very well that you can. Rishis do marry. No. I am not asking for that. That is too much to expect. Too much of commitment. All I am asking, requesting and begging is that I bear your son. That's all I want in my life. I don't want anything more.”

“You only want my son?” Richika was astonished.

"Yes, Rishis are permitted to give a son to a woman who desires and wishes for it."

Richika was spellbound. Each of her words carried her love, sincerity, conviction and courage. He was not only completely overwhelmed by her beauty but also by her brilliance. At that moment, rationality and irrationality merged into one. He too wanted her. He simply wanted her as much as she did. He got up and stretched his arms towards her. She kept the lamp in the window sill and flowed into his arms. Her destiny fulfilled, she became love. It was a strange night for the Rishi and the girl.

He said, "I am not a great prospect for a husband either!"

"What you do mean?"

"I am going progressively blind. I have to finish so much of learning by reading. Sage Kashyapa says, it is only a matter of time before I go totally blind."

The girl's eyes filled with tears of love. She said, "Hush. Nothing will happen. If it does—your son will be there as your eyes. His eyes will be your eyes!"

Richika laughed, "At heart you are still a silly girl. How do you know you will have a child—that too a son? One unguarded event does not necessarily mean you will have a son."

She said calmly, "I will. You will see. But don't worry, I am not going to ask you to marry me when I have my son. The only condition is that I should have a son."

"What are you talking about? You need a father for the child too, if you have to have a child."

"Women from time immemorial have brought up their

children on their own. Don't you bother about it."

Richika fell asleep bereft of any thoughts of guilt in the languid mood, enveloped by her total love. At four in the morning the woman, girl no longer, got up. Looked at the handsome face of the man she loved, picked up the rudraksha beads next to his pallet, touched his feet so lightly that it did not waken him. She blew off the oil lamp. She walked out, shutting the door gently. She went to the old man, touched his feet and said, "I keep my promise, Tata" and left.

On the side of the Ganga, Kashyapa sat in meditation as usual. She wondered "Who will sweep his yard now?" and walked away. Once out of sight of Kashyapa, she bathed and prayed to the Ganga and told her, "Maa! Please give me Richika's son! That is all I want. Nothing else—ever!"

Moving On With Blessings

Before Vatsayani, who now called herself Ganga, moved away from Haridwar, she sat beside the river Ganga and asked herself, "What do I do next?" In the past few months, while doing the chores of sweeping Sage Kashyapa's courtyard, she often sat behind the pillars, observing him offering advice to pregnant women and children. She absorbed every word like the parched earth drinks up raindrops falling before the monsoons; not a drop wasted, not a word wasted.

He was telling a pregnant woman, probably a very wealthy one, judging by the silks she was draped in and gorgeous jewellery around her neck, arms, wrists and waist, yet to be thickened by the baby she was carrying. On her ankles glistened anklets of gold. Must be a queen or at least a princess. There were several attendants with her. She was saying, "I want a son fit to be a king!" Kashyapa smiled and said, "All mothers want that!"

She said, "I will do anything to achieve it!" Kashyapa said, "Yes, you could do some good things so that the baby grows up healthy in the physical and psychological sense." Then he started his discourse. Ganga was all ears, even more than the wealthy woman. Ganga even wondered if the sage had some inkling of what she was planning.

"You see, the foetus is alive from the time of conception. I have already told you how to worship Gods, Brahmins and nature and eat the right kind of food. You have the thoughts of your husband and his good qualities when you join him in this sacred task of creating this baby.

"After that, all the nine months you need to practise similar rituals and austerities to lead a good life. You should not have bad thoughts, see bad people or ungainly objects or hear of sad events. You should surround yourself with good people, sacred chants or music and be clean, wear good clothes, so that the baby is surrounded by a good environment."

The princess said, "Yes—I will do that. But how can an unborn baby be affected by what I do?" Kashyapa says, "In the foetus, the flesh develops from the maternal component. All the major and minor parts of the body develop from the mother, father, *satmya* (congenials) *rasa* (nutrients), *satva* (psyche) and *atma* (self), along with the actions of the five elements, earth, water, fire, air and sky as smelled, tasted, seen, touched and heard by the five senses.

"In the third month, all the body parts manifest simultaneously and the foetus quivers, achieves consciousness and feels pain. In the third month the mind also is more manifest than the sense organs.

"In the fourth month, the foetus gets stability and becomes free from abnormalities. Because of this, the pregnant woman experiences heaviness of the body."

The princess nodded, accepting that she too felt heavy though she did not look it. She simply looks so perfect, Ganga thought admiringly.

Kashyapa said, "Now the foetus is stable, without complications. There are less chances of abnormalities and miscarriages.

"But in the fifth month, there is increase in the blood flow and flesh in the foetus. You will look emaciated but I assure you, you will be fine. You are just feeding the little one more."

The princess was happy, yet naturally a little scared too. "So I assure you, my girl that you will have an uneventful pregnancy. Now leading a good life is left to you."

Ganga, at that moment, felt that she lived within the body of the princess. A virgin, yet she was joyously pregnant!

Kashyapa continued, "In the sixth month, there is increase in strength and *ojas* (vital power) and of course the mother will be more tired and will have sallow complexion."

"In the seventh month, the foetus will be complete in all respects with all *dhatus* and limbs along with optimum levels of *vata*, *pitta* and *kapha*. The woman, thus, feels always tired. In the eighth month, the *ojas* exchange between the mother and the foetus occurs. The little one is a great trickster." Kashyapa laughed. "He tries to cheat the mother and draws more *ojas* from her. It is not a fair exchange; so the mother swings between happiness and languor. Because of this imbalance, it is not a good month for the baby to be born."

"Finally, in the ninth month, the infant is born. The foetus remembers all the deeds of the previous life as well as the sorrows and happiness of the mother's womb—but only till he gets his new life at birth."

Kashyapa then added, musing almost to himself, "According to Charaka, when psyche (mind) is dominated by *satva*, then the child remembers his pervious life but when associated with *rajas* and *tamas*, he does not remember his past. I wonder if it is true. I don't know! It is said that if he is a healer, he will always remember his past births!"

Ganga told herself with conviction, "My child will be a healer and he will remember everything!" As if she just had to wish it, and it would come true!

The princess asked, "What food should I take? What drinks may I have safely so that my baby flourishes and is not harmed?"

Kashyapa asked her, "Are you going to feed the baby or is the wet nurse?"

The princess blushed and bent her head. "The master would not like me to lose my beauty. So it will have to be a wet nurse. But I will see to it that she is cleansed before feeding my precious one." Kashyapa frowned, perhaps at the vanity, lack of concern and the ignorance. Even animals feed their young ones. But then, he, being a man, what could he know? Even Ganga had not heard of mothers who do not feed their babies!

Finally he said, "Your home must be filled with music—singing, flute and veena should be played. Even good story recitations to bc welcomed. The unborn ought to be able to differentiate complex swaras and ragas.

"Your home must be clean, fumigated, free from mosquitoes or insects. There should be burning fire. Bathe in clean boiled water and cleanse with split pea flour. Bathe in a protected place to avoid infections. Wear soft clothes. Have food specially made of twenty five types of grains."

The princess and her attendants paid close attention to what the sage was saying.

He continued, "For the kind of ideal child you hope for, for example one with fair complexion, virile, pious and for longevity—you should take the flour of parched white barley with honey and ghee. It should be mixed with milk of a white cow with white live calf, churned in a pot of silver or even bronze. You should eat 'sali' rice, white barley, milk, curds and ghee."

"You should adorn yourself always in good clothes and ornaments. You should also look at a white horse and a bull in the morning and evening."

The princess and the attendants paid obeisance to the sage and laid a silken purse of silver coins tied with silk strings at his feet and left.

When he was alone, he called out, "Girl! Come here." Ganga was terrified. This meant he was aware she was snooping all this time. She went to him timidly and touched his feet. She spoke in chaste Sanskrit. "I am sorry. I apologise."

He smiled and patted her head. "It is okay. Gaining knowledge is no sin but wallowing in ignorance is! Here take this, it will be of use to you in the days to come," and handed her the silken purse of silver.

"Your holiness! I should not—I must not."

"Consider it payment for the courtyard swept!" He smiled. Ganga was dumbfounded. She knew he was the best healer of children in the world. But she had not known he had the *jnana chaksu* (divine vision). Humbly, she touched his feet and left with the silken purse tucked to her waist.

Her heart lifted. She knew that he knew what was in her heart. He just gave his stamp of approval.

As Ganga sat on the rock with her feet dangling in water, her mind went back to the day when the sage had given her the silken purse and had entered into conspiracy with her to fulfill her only ambition to have a scholarly son. He had given all the instructions and now it was up to her to put it into practice. It would have been easy for the princess, but would it be possible for her? She had to explore all the possibilities to see that her conceived, yet unborn, got everything he deserved.

There was not an iota of doubt that he would come into being. In a month's time, it would be proven.

She said to herself, "First of all, I should no longer walk in the nights. I am not a vagabond. I am a married woman, married the Gandharva way. I no longer have my man with me, but I should behave as if he is there." She wondered where she should go now. Perhaps to Rishikesh. She stopped a wandering sadhu. "Sir, how far is Rishikesh? Could you show me the way?"

He said, "Lone woman—you should not go by yourself—I am walking that way. You can follow me, but I am celibate. Don't get wrong ideas!"

Ganga's eyes filled with tears, she bowed and touched his feet, "Swamiji, I am eternally grateful to you. I am a devoted wife, whose husband is called away. He will come to Rishikesh in the coming months." Ganga was not lying. If only he knew, he would come.

The sanyasi opened his bundle and took out a clean length of saffron fabric. "Cover yourself with this, so that no one looks at you in an unholy way." Gratefully, Ganga took the fabric and wrapped herself. The sadhu stopped and offered oblations to the Ganga and then they took the path amidst the forests to Rishikesh. The sadhu was an elderly man and frail. They covered ten miles on the first day, steadily walking, ten on the second and ten on the third day.

When they reached Rishikesh, she told him, "I cannot tell you how grateful I am."

He said "There are ashrams here where you can stay. Some

are very generous and don't even ask how long you will stay. You can await your husband here. My blessings are with you," and walked away. Before she could collect herself to thank him, he had already disappeared in thick foliage on the side of the Ganga.

She was feeling hot and dusty. She had not bathed for three days. She could not, for fear of offending her travel companion. She started remembering Sage Kashyapa's instructions: "Well, I need to clean up and dress better." She went to the little shop on the banks where all the auspicious materials for worship were being sold. She asked the shopkeeper for a white fabric made of bark of the trees. He looked askance. This sanyasin—what had she gotten into her head? "It costs a silver. It is sacred and precious and costs a lot. You cannot afford it, sanyasin." Ganga quietly took her silken purse and gave him the coin. Surprised, he picked up the fabric, folded it and put it on her extended palm. She said, "Some ghee, parched grams and sali rice." He pointed to another store, "You will get those there!" Ganga took the fabric and went to a sheltered cove on the Ganga and bathed in the river, simultaneously offering her prayers. When she finished her bath she wore the white saree, washed her old saree and the saffron fabric too. It might come handy in the days to come. Barley and rice could wait till she was sure. But white flowers, they were in abundance in the forests. She picked some, wove them with their own stems and draped them on her hair. She felt good! Now I am rightfully going to be the divine mother!

She sat down to think "I need to surround myself with music, sacred verses and good people. Rishikesh, like Varanasi, is known for such things. There are ashrams and kutirs of sadhus all along. I need to find myself a place suitable for both of us." She was listing out the possibilities. She might be better off, staying in places where there were women. After all, there were women ascetics. They might be compassionate and offer her shelter. Women ascetics are found among the four major castes. There are also other devout groups called Linginis that belonged to the Baudha sect, Jain sect, Vaishnavas, Shaiva, Shakta faith and those who wandered and those living in temples and serving. The last two would not do for her. Even the working class had Karukis, recognised by their professions. Women of all castes and sects intermingled freely, including eating and sleeping together, exchanging garlands, clothes and so on. But she had a few needs. She had to wear white, eat barley, rice, ghee and drink milk. She first would have to seek shelter. Thus began her exploration for a home.

The Sanctuary

She walked along the narrow crooked street looking for a place of refuge. There were tiny huts, cottages, shacks and modest ashrams facing the street, yet all had a large vista of the Ganga and the hills beyond and snowy mountains far, far away.

As she walked, she heard melodious singing of soulful bhajans. She stopped and hesitated at the gate. An old woman beckoned her, "Come, everyone is welcome here!"

Ganga walked in fearfully, head down and eyes downcast and joined a motley crowd of men and women swaying to the drumbeats and listening to the sublime music. She sat transfixed. When the bhajan got over, the Swamiji, a man in his sixties with an impressive physique, covered in saffron cloth and a saffron head cover, did the arti, brought it around and handed over some puffed rice with pieces of jaggery as prasad. Ganga touched his feet and took the prasad, after touching the eyes with warmed fingers from the arti flame.

Then, one by one the people assembled left. Only the old woman was there. Ganga asked her, "May I stay here the night? I have no place to go." The old woman said, "Of course, you can. This is a safe haven for a destitute. But Swamiji goes begging for his food. I get by picking roots and fruits in the forest. We live frugally, we have nothing. But we will share what we have."

Ganga said, "I am grateful for your help, mother. I just need a safe place. I have little money, I could buy some grains, I can cook and clean. I won't be in your way." Then she shyly added, "I would love to learn to sing like the Swamiji."

The old woman laughed aloud, "Did you hear that, Swamiji? She wants to learn to sing. You have got yourself a much-needed disciple to pass on your music." The Swamiji smiled, "Why not? She does the chores and in return I teach her to pray to Goddess Saraswathi. It is night time, time for you to get some rest, Maa!" The old woman said, "I do look forward to it. I am really tired. I am not complaining. You have been so kind to me, but I am getting on in years." She led Ganga to a tiny room with one wooden pallet which was obviously where she slept. "Come, you can sleep on the pallet" — a generous soul she was. Ganga demurred. "No, no, a mat or a chaddar would do for me. I won't be a bother. I will sleep in the corner here. The old woman took a chaddar and a blanket and gave it to her. "If you are hungry, I can give you puffed rice." Ganga gratefully ate the leftover puffed rice and quenched her thirst with water.

They both went to sleep. As the old woman snored gently, Ganga fell into deep sleep after many uncertain days and restless nights.

She was up at four. She bathed and prayed to the Ganga and came and started her first chore of sweeping of the yard. That's when she saw in the early dawn a silvery white cow, with her young calf. Ganga's heart leapt with joy. "A cow. A white cow. My God! A white cow!" The old lady had forgotten to tell her they had one. Ganga went to the riverside, picked some green grass, filled the bucket next to the cow with water and fed the cow. As the cow contentedly chewed the grass, Ganga rubbed the cow's back and forehead. Ganga felt more content than she had ever felt since she had left her home and the old life behind. They too had cows back home. The calf was hungry. Ganga went back and found a couple of pails in the little kitchen, milked the cow, left the calf to feed and brought the warm and frothy milk to the ashram. She made the fire in the clay stove with dry twigs. It was easy as the cinders from the previous day still lay dormant. As the milk was about to boil over, she used the pallu of her saree to lift it off.

It was still dark. The old woman came. She was pleased to see the girl up and attending to the chores. She said, "I cannot milk that cow. So, I just leave the calf to feed. The calf must be angry with you for stealing her milk but, I for one, am happy to have some milk for ourselves."

"I could make curds and get butter and buttermilk." The old woman sighed contentedly. "Oh, to have buttermilk once again on a hot summer's day!"

Life settled into a happy routine. Swamiji was bound to his ritual begging, but did not insist that the womenfolk do the same. They were not ascetics. But when offered the milk or something they cooked, he took it in his kamandal and ate it. Food was not an important thing in his life but music was. He also kept some time aside to teach Ganga the rudiments of music.

On one occasion he said, "You have the talent and a divine voice, you deserve better." He went into his portion of the ashram where the women never entered even to clean up, and came back with a beautiful tanpura with ivory inlays and beads attached to the strings at the end. He tuned it, saying, "It gets better if you play it regularly. There is nothing like the four strings to produce heavenly music!" He handed it to her. She was astonished. "Me, I am a novice. I may damage it. It is too precious. Please Swamiji." Swamiji said, "My girl, the owner of the tanpura is no longer in this world. He would have been happy to give it to you. Please play on it. It is yours for now." He started teaching her to play and sing at the same time. When she first played the four strings, her head filled with music. She closed her eyes and gently strummed. She was in a different world. The Swamiji was bemused by her ecstasy. He smiled at the old woman as if to say, "Look who has come into our humble abode!" The old woman saw Saraswathi resplendent in her white saree play the tanpura. She even thought she saw heavy gold jewellery of four strands on her neck. She must be imagining it. But white flowers were certainly there. She wondered when the girl had time to string flowers with the many chores she had taken over.

The days passed. One night, as they were about to sleep, Ganga saw the full moon outside gleaming and reflected in the Ganga. She muttered, "Soon I will know!" "What?" said the old woman who was almost asleep. "Oh, something I need to know" and started saying her prayers. The old drowsy woman was soothed by the prayers and thought, "She is such a good devout girl. I hope she stays with us. She has such a soothing and caring presence."

A week passed. Two weeks. Ganga's joy knew no bounds. It was going to be a son, she knew that. The old woman was not stupid. One day she asked Ganga, "Are you married? Are you pregnant?" Ganga said, "Mother. I am married and pregnant. I am helpless. I have to manage on my own. God knows for how long. Please don't tell Swamiji. He may not like the idea at all of my staying." The old woman said, "He is a realised soul. None of this matters to him. You can stay here as long as I am there. But it won't be right if I am not here!"

Ganga was alarmed, "But you are here, you are not going anywhere, are you?"

The old woman stroked her cheeks kindly and said, "I

don't mean going away temporarily. I meant when Lord Yama decides that my time is up. After all, I am eighty years old. It is almost time to depart."

Ganga hugged her and said, "I have found a mother at last. Please don't leave me now. I need you."

"I know that, my child. But these things are not in our hands. Count your blessings. The one in your womb now is in a wonderful place of spirituality and beauty. Who knows what the future will bring? I admire you, my girl, living in this hovel with little worldly possessions, yet you are joyous. Being happy is the greatest gift one can have!"

Days and nights passed uneventfully, punctuated by blissful moments. Ganga would go with the old woman to the forest to look for roots and fruits when she was free. The forest was her source of ecstasy. As she entered the forests, she could feel the forest spirits entering her. She would feel the green glory entering her, filling her up with the chirping of the crickets in unison, the bird songs offering the music for her soul. Whenever she saw something beautiful, she became it. Only the other day she saw a silver grey tree beautifully dancing, with bright orange blossoms on each branch covering it fully, creating an orange splendour. Ganga was that tree at that moment. When she saw a herd of deer as they shimmered—moved silently—she was them. Even when she went closer, they never moved away. Or took flight out of fear.

Ganga had always believed that River Ganga was her mother where she felt at home, at all moments of fury and joy. The forest was different. It was pure joy.

She whispered to her son, "Don't you enjoy this beauty of nature?" She smiled as he kicked, to show that he agreed with her.

The old woman asked curiously, "Who are you talking to?" Ganga smiled and pulled her hand towards her abdomen and said "Him!"

The old woman smiled, "Him? You already know?" Ganga smiled, "Of course. His name is Jivaka!"

Old woman laughed uproariously. "He is yet unborn and you have a name for him! You are a crazy girl! I have never seen anyone like you. But you are a good girl. I pray for you and Jivaka."

Then one evening around the seventh month of Jivaka's life, during the bhajans in the evenings, the old woman slumped down and was no more. There was a hush and the Swamiji's eyes rested on the old body. He said "Good woman! She deserves a good death," and stood up.

He told the group, "One of you please take Ganga home. Tomorrow, please come at dawn and help me with the cremation."

Ganga was weeping silently. The women surrounded her and patted her. "You should not weep now at this stage. Come with us."

Out In The Open

Ganga's sheltered, happy life came to an end. She knew it as she watched the funeral pyre of the old woman, who was her mother for seven months. The Ganga flowed smoothly, eventually taking even the ashes away.

As she returned to the ashram to bid goodbye to her music teacher and protector, she made her belongings into a bundle and went and touched his feet. "I am truly grateful for what you have done for me. Now it is time for me to go. Old mother had warned me of this eventuality. But I am grateful...Jivaka and I are grateful for providing us this heavenly sanctuary!"

Swamiji stood up and said, "There is no need for you to

go. I have been planning to go to Gangotri and spend the rest of my life in meditation there. Having given shelter to the old mother, I could not abandon her. Your coming was good for her. You stay here as long as you can. I say that because I see dark clouds surrounding you. I pray for you. May Ganga be your protector till you complete the journey you have set yourself."

He gathered his rolled blanket, picked up his kamandal and set out. Then he turned back and pointed, "If things become unbearable here, go to the mountain beyond. The shrine Neelakanta is there, entrenched in the thousand-year-old banyan roots. There are Shakta women ascetics who live there. They may appear harsh, but they are good souls. Tell them that Shivananda sent you. They will take care of you."

Ganga was stunned. His mind was made up. She settled into a quiet routine, as if both the old woman and Swamiji were there. She was constantly talking to Jivaka, telling him everything that happened. She continued her music. But people no longer came to the ashram. She knew that there was change in the air. Then she heard voices of women outside the window. "Look at this whore—the harlot. She came here seven months back and she is pregnant. Swamiji was a good man. She ruined him by seducing him. The old woman was blind as a bat, bless her soul. She did not know what was going on behind her back. Swamiji was a good man but a weak one!"

Within two days an angry man came and knocked at the door. When she opened the door he said, "This land and hut were given to the Swamiji by my father thirty years ago for his use. Not for the use of a harlot. The milk cow was given last year by my uncle. You have no place here!" and walked away. Thank heavens, they did not physically harm her. That was the most important thing.

For the third time in her brief life, she packed her belongings, covered herself with the saffron cloth and left her sanctuary at four in the morning.

Before she left, she hugged the calf and the cow she had named Mangala. "Mangala, you have been good to me and Jivaka. I am very grateful. I pray to Gangamayya that you and your baby may live happy and forever!"

The cow sensed that this kind, loving soul too was going away. Her tears dropped and mingled with Ganga's tears. "I must not cry. It upsets Jivaka if I do—I better go!" She released the calf to feed and walked away, without a backward glance, into the morning mist.

The path to Neelakanta was not a very steep climb. But in the eighth month of pregnancy, it was not easy. She was strong and fit. She recalled Kashyapa's words. "Eighth month is month of turmoil—between depression and ecstasy. The foetus draws *ojas* from the mother. She has to be very careful." Ganga sighed, "I am doing my best, Jivaka!"

It was almost night when she reached the Neelakanta shrine. Ganga prayed to Neelakanta, who held the poison in his throat to protect the universe—to see to the safety of Jivaka. "The scriptures say a son sees to the passage to heaven of his father. But they don't say that for the mother. In fact, the mother is immortal because she lives in her son. Jivaka, make me immortal," she prayed. It was dark everywhere. She could barely see the shrine.

She lay down under the tree and fell asleep with exhaustion. In the early hours of the morning, she thought she was dreaming —three demonesses were peering at her. Her brain cleared. Oh! The Shakta ascetics! She got up, heaved and bent to touch their feet. They had tridents in their hands and matted hair. Their faces were decorated with ash and vermillion. But she had no fear! Swamiji had assured her that they were good souls.

"Who are you? Why are you here at such an advanced stage of pregnancy? This is not the place for a pregnant woman!"

Ganga simply said, "Swami Shivananda said that you will give me shelter. It is just for a month."

"You silly woman. We are ascetics. We have nothing but prayers. How can we look after you or provide for you?"

"All I need is your prayers, mothers. I am tough. I can feed myself and my Jivaka."

"Who is Jivaka?" They were curious to know.

"He is the yet-to-be-born!"

"You speak a good tongue. Well educated, from a good family. What do you know about Jivaka? From where did you get this name?"

"Mother! I don't know. My father and Jivaka's father are scholars."

"Are they alive?"

"Yes!"

"Then why are they not with you in this hour of need?"

"Perhaps—it is meant to be that way!"

The ascetics were scholars. "You don't know the meaning of Jivaka and you still have named the unborn baby by that name. How did you find the name? Do you know its meaning?"

"No, mothers, I don't."

"Well, in the *Vishnu Purana* it is said that the person who is a survivor and who defies all adversities and diseases and even old age is called Jivaka."

"Is that so? This explains the name I heard in my dream!"

The ascetics were curious about this strange pregnant woman.

"What dream?"

"In my dream, I saw a five-year-old child running into the Ganga in the middle of a cold winter morning. The top layer of the Ganga shimmered with frozen ice. The boy was fair, beautiful with long curly black hair up to his shoulders. He was wearing a white thin cloth wrapped around him. As he ran towards the water, I heard the voice crying out, 'No. Jivaka—No, No—Don't do it!' The voice was that of Sage Kashyapa whom I have met and spoken to. I knew that he was going to protect Jivaka and I had no fear in my heart! Then I woke up. I knew that Jivaka is going to be with Sage Kashyapa and will always be protected." She smiled contently. The ascetics were dumbfounded.

The three ascetics started discussing amongst themselves

and finally said, "It is alright, child. You can stay here and serve Neelakanta. No one will hurt you when we are here but we know nothing about caring for pregnant women. If you can manage yourself, we are fine with that. We will give you powerful spiritual protection and see no harm comes to your baby. But we cannot guarantee the same for you."

"Thank you, mothers! I am truly grateful. That is all the assurance I need."

In spite of their fierce looks and rough speech, they were child-like in their behaviour. They were awkward around her, trying to find things for her to eat or drink that were suitable. They were Shaktas and ate meat and drank and smoked bhang till they went into a stupor. When intoxicated, they indulged in all sorts of rituals. Ganga, on the other hand, prayed to Neelakanta and to the Ganga gleaming below as seen from the top, the precipice. But she was calm and felt protected. Those four weeks were the most uncomfortable, when Ganga found it hard to sit or lie down, sometimes even to breathe. One of the ascetics showed her how to relax her body and to breathe deeply so that she could rest.

One day they came to where she was sitting watching the sun set and said, "There is a problem. There is a Kumbha mela in Kanakhala. We have to go there. It is an obligation. We cannot abandon you at the mountaintop all alone, nor can you trudge to Kanakhala with us! What shall we do? We have heard though that there is a washerwoman several miles upstream on the Ganga above Rishikesh, toward Uttarakashi, who acts as a midwife. She has even delivered babies in the King's palace when his own physician could not handle the delivery."

"Mothers, the time for me has come to seek that woman. I will go my way and find her. I will find her. Please don't worry on my account. Please go to the Kumbha mela."

The four women set forth. Three went down to Kanakhala and one went up towards Uttarkashi. When she saw the silhouette of the palace above, Ganga knew that she was somewhere near the place of safety.

This is when hell broke loose. A sudden storm swept the river and the mountains. Branches of trees were breaking and falling, so one could not even take shelter under a tree. Lightning filled the sky with blue streaks. It was freezing cold. Rain clouds melted into torrents of water. For the first time in her young life, Ganga was scared. She prayed, "Gangamayya, make me immortal by giving Jivaka his life!"

Her prayers rose to a frenzy. She kept crying out to Ganga to protect her baby.

Finally...

Gangamayya's Fury

Neela, the midwife and washerwoman, hurried to catch the boat. She had just handed over the bundle of washed clothes at the master's house and was rushing home. Dark clouds had gathered, portents of a brewing storm. Gangamayya was angry. She could be brutal and lethal when she was angry. The boatman was already pulling the boat up. Neela ran to him begging, "Bhayya, please take me across. Gangamayya is too angry for me to swim across. I live in the shack yonder. We may have to move upcountry soon. Gangamayya is rising rapidly."

The boatman said, "I am sorry, but I too have to get home, on this side."

Neela begged, "I have a husband, four daughters and four boys waiting, the youngest is only six months old. Left the boy with the eldest girl. We needed the money from the clothes washed. Please, Bhayya!" He drew the boat back into the water, "Hurry up, one more trip won't make a difference." He added, "I am only a bachelor!"

Neela added, "May Gangamayya bless you for this charity. May be she blesses you with a good wife too."

She sighed, "Who knows what awaits across the other side. My family may have already moved to safety. My kids—they deserve the best."

Soon they were swiftly moving across the river. When she tried to pay him on reaching the other side, he refused. "This is my gift, sister," and pushed off. Breathless, and in a hurry, holding the coins tied to her saree pallu, she started running towards her home. The Ganga was roaring. The trees were swaying, thunder clapping, lightning striking everywhere without ceasing. With prayers to Gangamayya on her lips, she ran. A strong woman, a good woman, whose strong arms birthed many a village woman. She was a much sought-after midwife. Suddenly she heard a moan. She would have recognised it anywhere. Like a mother for her infant, like a cow for her calf—she was attuned to pick it up from a medley of noises of Gangamayya's fury. "Hey Gangamayya! Can it be true? The moan of a birthing woman!" She forgot about her family. She was now the earth mother. She ran towards the low, mewing sound.

She found under a tree, drenched, a young beautiful woman—pale as ivory, obviously in pain. Neela crouched. The woman, no more than 16, as young as her eldest daughter. But obviously a Brahmin.

The woman cried out, "Help me, mother!"

Neela said, "How can I touch you, I am a woman of low birth, a mere washerwoman!"

The young woman said, "There are no low births. Even a washerwoman is an ascetic, a 'lingini'."

"I know, I can help you. How can I leave you here amidst the storm under a tree? No woman deserves it! Oh God, oh Gangamayya! What am I to do?"

The young woman spoke clearly. "There is no greater sin than denying help to a birthing woman—Brahmin or not!"

Neela told her, "My hovel is here. I don't know how long it will stand. Gangamayya is rising rapidly. Soon she will devour what was my home. But now you are my daughter. I will take you with me."

The woman gave a wan smile. "I will come with you, Maa. My soul will always bless you for bringing out my son to this glorious earth!"

Neela wondered, "Obviously educated and abandoned. Not even a dog deserves this fate!" She lifted her. She was light as a child. She was indeed a child! "She weighs as much as a palm full of jasmine flowers!" Neela sighed as she stooped down and lifted her.

As she carried her, she asked, "Who are you? Where are your parents or husband? How could anyone do this to you?"

The woman said, "It is all my doing—it is for my son. You know what his name is. It is Jivaka!"

"Yet to be born—you already know it is a boy and that too you have already named him! You are amazing!"

Neela heard her daughter shouting, "Maa, come fast, we are leaving. We are going to the higher and safer place. Come, come!" She came running and when she saw the burden her mother carried, she was aghast. "Maa, father and children have already taken all the things from our home and he sent me back to accompany you. What are you doing?"

"My child, if she were to be you, will I leave you to die under a tree?"

"Maa...but?"

"No buts, my child. I will have to deliver the baby and bring them with me. Tell me where you are heading, I will follow you. I promise you that Gangamayya has allotted me this duty."

"Maa! Okay, remember that we too need you. We are heading to the temple in the next hill. The Shiva temple you once took me to when I was small."

"You hurry, I can manage!" Neela added.

Neela took the young woman to her hut. There was nothing but a couple of old mats, some rags and earthen pots. Neela laid her on the mat. Fortunately, the hearth smouldered with cinders. She collected the pots outside, catching rainwater, lighted the fire and set the water boiling.

After lighting the lone oil lamp of clay, she dipped her hands in the warm mustard oil and gently massaged the young woman's low back, saying soothingly, "I am praying for the birth of a healthy baby" and repeatedly saying, "It is going to be perfectly all right, my child. I am here with you!" The young woman's body relaxed and her mind was at ease. It was as if at death's door, she had found heaven.

Neela heard the young woman praying to Prajapathi, Indra, Indrani and Aswini Kumaras, the divine medicine men. Neela was astounded. Who was this girl? How could she know these prayers uttered in chaste Sanskrit?

The contractions were coming more swiftly. The woman was burning with fever. Neela laid a cold wet rag on her forehead. The woman said, "Please remember everything I say, Maa. I will not be here much longer."

"Hush..child!"

"No, Maa, I know. Gangamayya is calling. My task on earth is over. Please listen.

"When my son is born, note the time. Ask the temple priest to write the time. His name is Jivaka, his father Richika and I the mother, Vatsayani! Can you remember?"

"Yes, yes, now push…push…!"

"Then I will give you this gold chain. Please take care of Jivaka—and use this. I know you are poor and have many children."

"Okay, okay. Now…push…"

She was not screaming like other women. She was using her strength to talk.

"When Jivaka is three or four, when you think fit, please take him to Kanakhala. There on the banks of Ganga, you will find Sage Kashyapa. He is out meditating at four in the mornings, summer or winter. Tell him this orphan child is his to care for. Don't worry, he is a healer of children. He will not refuse."

Neela said, "I am a simple washerwoman. How can I do all these things?"

"Never mind. Just give the *Bhojpatra* with Jivaka and his parents' names written on it and say that it was the boy's mother's dying wish that he too will become a healer of children. He is destined to be one!"

Neela almost shouted, "It is a boy! It is a boy!" The woman had a blissful smile, though she was pale, as death had already taken over.

Neela found the baby in her hands and said wonderingly, "It is a boy." She put him on a rag near the fire after cutting his umbilical cord. When she came back, the woman was holding the necklace and thrust it into her hands. She was haemorrhaging badly and was sinking. Neela put the boy to her breasts. The woman gave a brilliant smile. "Thank you Maa, for giving me Jivaka. Now I can go in peace. Please take him and go to your family. Gangamayya will take care of me."

With a feeble attempt to touch the baby, she simply slipped away. Neela closed the woman's eyes. She went smiling peacefully, no pain of birthing showed on her face.

Neela took the baby, quickly cleaned him up by the fire, wrapped him in a rag and laid him on a mat. She went and covered the body and whispered, "Gangamayya give me the wisdom and strength to care for this divine child." When she turned, she saw the infant with open eyes, turning and looking at the fire. He then turned and looked at her. He had a birthmark on his left shoulder. Similar to the one his mother had on her left shoulder. Not a whimper, not a cry or drowsy unconsciousness of a newborn. She had never ever seen one bright and alert like this one. His dark silken ringlets shone in the light of the fire.

She muttered, "Jivaka—the divine infant—come home to me." She took the baby and virtually ran all the way to the Shiva temple.

The family gathered around her. The girls exclaimed, "What a beautiful baby."

Her own six-month-old was crying with hunger. Her milk flowed. She fed both of them. Jivaka was no learner. He sucked like a seasoned feeder! Neela just could not get over it. There was one secret though. She never showed the necklace to anyone. It would be a temptation for her poor family. She hid it, to be given to Jivaka in his mother's memory.

The husband was worried about the new home to be built. Neela asked him, "Are you angry that I brought home another mouth to feed?" He said, "Gangamayya guides you. I am a mere mortal. I have never seen you doing anything wrong. You are a good woman and I am proud of you. No other woman would have done what you did today."

Those words brought tears in her eyes. "You are all I have —but Gangamayya orders me to do things—and it is hard for you all to deal with it. But I love you all till my dying day. Now there is one more too!"

When Gangamayya subsided, life returned to normal. On the eleventh day, Neela bundled Jivaka and took him to the Ganga temple. She sat outside at dawn waiting for the priest to finish the morning arti for Gangamayya. He walked to her, "You are the washerwoman. What are you doing here at this hour?"

"Swamiji, please don't tell anyone, I found this baby the evening Gangamayya breached the banks and entered this temple and demolished the hovel there. To tell you the truth, I did not find this baby. I birthed this baby. The young woman, obviously a Brahmin, died during the birth. She made me promise to care for this baby. She insisted that I should keep the record of his birth. She asked me to ask you to write on a Bhoj leaf all the details. I am supposed to give it to his foster parents if I can find them." Neela did not want to mention Sage Kashyapa's name. Already, the priest was frowning with puzzlement.

"And also today is the eleventh day. Please name him too after offering a prayer. I have a gold coin. I will give it to you."

"Foolish woman. What would I do with a gold coin? I will name the boy and cast his horoscope."

"Name?"

"Jivaka."

"Mother's name?"

"Vatsa... Vatsa..."

"Vatsala? Vatsayani?"

"Yes, the second one."

"Father's name?"

"Richika."

"Time?"

"Eleven days back, before you moved to higher grounds, you rang the temple bells. The mother and I both heard it."

"All right!"

He recited some mantras—kept the baby on his lap and named him Jivaka. "He belongs to Brugu Gothra," he declared! "Yes" Neela agreed, though she did not know what it meant. He rolled the Bhoj leaf and kept it under the beams of the temple.

"Take it whenever you plan to give the boy away." He tickled the baby's feet. "He is a lovely baby. Don't change your mind and keep him with you permanently!" He teased.

Neela said, "One more thing, Swamiji. This is a Brahmin baby. We are illiterate Shudras. His mother seemed very educated and noble. I want him to grow up in a better environment. I have seen you spending the whole day here and sleeping the nights here. Can I bring him here when he starts walking? He needs a better environment than what I or my big family can give. Please Swamiji, I believe that he is a divine child placed under my care!"

The priest wondered. Who knows the ways of Gangamayya?

That the baby survived the night of her fury itself was a miracle. If she wished he should help this poor woman, so be it. Who knew what this child was?

He simply said, "I am an old man. If he is not naughty, it's okay. If he can learn something I can teach, may it be so!"

Neela was overwhelmed by his kindness. She touched his feet and thanked him "One final question? Is it a sin that a low caste woman like me birthed this baby and am now taking care of him, feeding him my milk?"

The priest said, "Caste is a creation of man. Mother's love is divine. Have no fear. No harm will come to you. In fact, for this good deed, Gangamayya will bless you and your family." He picked a flower from the arti plate, took out sacred water and poured it into her outstretched right palm.

Neela was shocked and delighted. No Brahmin priest had ever treated her with so much kindness. She once again touched his feet, picked up Jivaka and walked home. She felt light. The idea of sin had bothered her ever since she picked up Jivaka's mother in her arms.

The Midwife's Tale

Now that Neela had two babies, with six months between them, it was like having twins. Yadu and Jivaka were almost twins. Older kids used to tease the boys as 'Shukla Paskha' and 'Krishna Paksha'. Full moon and no moon because of their colouring. Not that they minded. They constantly played, bothered and loved each other. Neela's husband and entire family loved Jivaka. But by an unwritten consent from all, they never cooked any food of flesh, fowl or fish as long as Jivaka was part of their family.

As agreed with the priest of the Gangamayya temple, when Neela went about her washerwoman chores or midwifery calls, she left Jivaka at the temple. Believe it or not, he walked at seven months and spoke at nine months. Her own Yadu at one would take two steps and say two words. At those times, the priest spoke to him in chaste Sanskrit and taught him the worship of Ganga, arti and all. He was astounded at the rate at which the little fellow was picking up language, concepts and actions. He called the priest 'Tata' and for the priest, it was one of the best sounds he had heard in his lonely life of eighty six years.

When barely three, Jivaka was asking, "Tata, why does the sun rise? Where does he go at night?"

The priest, though knowing much about prayers and rituals, could not answer the little boy's questions. He would say, "You need to find a better teacher than me, Jivaka!"

Jivaka would come and hug him and say, "Tata, I don't want a better teacher. I want you to become one, so that I can always be with you!"

The priest's eyes filled with tears of love. He said to himself —it is time for the fledgling bird to fly. No matter how painful, this child deserves a better place. Neela was right in calling him a divine child.

It was one of the coldest winter nights. The family had decided to go to the car festival in the next village. Yadu was sniffling. He had a bad cold. Neela said, "We better not go. Yadu is not well." Jivaka said, "Maa, it's okay. You all go. I will stay with Yadu." Yadu said, "Yes, yes, we will play our secret games."

The eldest girl said, "It is okay, Maa, you go I will stay

with the boys."

So, the rest of the family went. Then suddenly in the middle of the night, Yadu could not breathe, he started choking. His sister, very frightened, said to Jivaka, "Jivaka, please be with him, I will call the priest for help. I will be back in a minute!" Minutes stretched into many more minutes. When the priest and the girl returned, it was an amazing sight.

Jivaka had carefully lifted the hot water pot from the stove, kept it down on the floor. He put in some leaves of Amritavalli, growing out on the path. He made Yadu sit near it and covered both of them, saying "I am making a tent for us. Now breathe! Now breathe!" As his breathing eased, Yadu started laughing. "Jivaka, this is a great game, let us play again." Jivaka was laughing too. The priest and the girl could not believe their eyes.

The girl said, "This is unbelievable. He is mostly like all other kids. Then suddenly you would think he is a grown up!"

The priest nodded. "Neela's divine child has to be found a better place than this: You know, Jivaka saved your brother's life. We would have been here too late!"

When Neela heard about it, she cried out, "My God" and held both Yadu and Jivaka and wept. Then she asked, "Jivaka, how did you know what to do?"

He said, "I saw you doing that when Didi was sick!"

"How did you lift the water pot with boiling water?"

"Like you do with a cloth—and it was only half-full—otherwise I would have taken out some, like you do!"

Neela said "Yes, you made it all so simple. But you are only three and a half, six months younger than Yadu—whose life you saved. Then she said, "Jivaka, your mother had told me that I will know when it is time for you to take you to Sage Kashyapa."

"My mother? You are my mother."

"No, Jivaka. I only brought you to this world. Your mother was the most beautiful and brave woman I have seen in my life."

"You say you are not my real mother. I believe you are. I never felt I am not of this family."

"Of course, you are. Your poor mother died even before she could feed you! I am also your and Yadu's mother."

"Maa, why should I go to Sage Kashyapa? Why cannot I live with you here?"

"Your mother wanted you to be a learned man. A scholar. What can we poor illiterate people give you?"

"But Tata teaches me. That's enough. I am happy here."

"No Jivaka, I have promised your mother as she lay dying that I will take you to Sage Kashyapa. Come, let us talk to Tata about this."

The priest said, "I have been of the same idea. Neela, I have taught him what I can. He tells me I should become a better teacher as he wants to stay with me. I know Neela, it is hard for us to let him go. But we both need to do that. We need to let him go. He has a great future ahead!"

Jivaka was silent. He was torn. If he insisted that he did not want to go, these two loving people would not force him. But they had their duties. He ought to allow them to fulfill it. Who knows what was in store for him? He would never be as happy as he was with Yadu as playmate. He sighed. "Yes, Maa. Yes, Tata. I will do what you say. It breaks my heart to leave you."

The priest hugged him and blessed him. "May you live a hundred years. May you be the *dipika*, shining light to the world and may you always be happy and content." That was the end of a chapter in Jivaka's life.

Neela travelled several days to reach Kanakhala. She reached the banks of Gangamayya. She waited through the night near the ashram of Kashyapa. As the young woman had predicted, the sage came and bathed in the river and sat under the peepal tree to meditate. Jivaka was asleep on her lap. As the sage finished his meditation at dawn, Neela bathed Jivaka in the river. She drew a little cloth bag from her waist and out come the shiny four-strand gold necklace. "Jivaka. This was your mother's. Keep it with you."

"Maa – you are my mother. It is yours."

"No, Jivaka No!"

"Maa, this is my gift to my sisters. I heard you talking to father about getting my sisters married. Break this up and get my sisters married. What do I need a necklace for?"

Neela broke down in tears. "Oh my divine child. Oh! My Jivaka."

"Now let me do what I promised your mother. It is getting harder by the minute." She tucked the jewellery bag back and took out the *Bhojpatra* document, walked to the sage, holding

Jivaka by the hand. They both touched Kashyapa's feet. He opened his eyes! Normally, people did not disturb him when he was in meditation. It was anyway time to start his day.

Neela said, "Your holiness, I am on a strange errand with even a stranger message. I am a poor washerwoman. If you don't help me, no one can. But I need to tell you a long story that happened more then three years ago!"

"But you have a child with you. Is it sick?"

"No, your holiness, he is not. But if he is, you could heal him."

Then she told him about Jivaka's mother and the instructions given by his mother. The child stood there quietly, taking in every word.

Then Neela gave him the *Bhojpatra* documents. "Jivaka's mother wanted me to give these details to you." Sage Kashyapa, through his divine vision, knew what was in it. Without looking, he put it in the little cloth bag in which he had placed his Rudraksha beads.

He just said, "All right, Jivaka, will you come with me?"

Jivaka said, "Yes, Guruji, but I want to say goodbye to my mother first."

As Kashyapa waited, Jivaka embraced Neela and said, "Thank you Maa. You are the best mother on earth. But please send Yadu to me when he is grown up, I want to come and see you wherever you are, when I am grown up. I will always remember you more than my real mother and mother Ganga! Goodbye." He kissed her and walked away.

Kashyapa stretched out his hand. Jivaka held it and they walked towards the ashram together. Jivaka asked, "May I call you Tata? I call the people I love Tata. I am sure I will come to love you. You are a kind man." Kashyapa, bemused, said, "But, of course."

Jivaka Comes Home

Holding on to the little boy's hand, Kashyapa came to the ashram, slowing his pace to allow little Jivaka to walk with him. Once he reached, the sage picked up a pot of water and kept it on the wood-fired earthen stove in the corridor.

Jivaka asked, "What is that for?"

Kashyapa said, "That is for your bath. I will help in bathing you."

Jivaka said, "I am big, I can take bath myself. I don't need hot water. I had my bath in the morning in the Ganga when you were having it, bathing a little farther away. My mother said I have to do all my chores myself and not to bother you as you are very busy. Are you busy?" He asked innocently.

Kashyapa "I am never too busy for you, my child. Now tell me what would you like to do? What did you do at home?"

Jivaka said, "In the morning after bath, mother gave us rotis to eat. After that we all played the whole day, except for two or three hours: I would go to the Ganga temple and learn the prayers with Tata. He would tell me nice stories of Ramayana and Mahabharatha. But he is getting old, finds it hard to do any work. He breathes hard even while fetching a pot of water from Ganga. So I take a smaller pot and fetch the water for him!" he sighed.

Kashyapa asked gently, "You miss them all already, don't you!"

"Yes, but Mother says this is where I need to be. Tata says that he has taught me all that he can. They both said, now onwards I have to learn from you. Will you please teach me what I need to know?"

Kashyapa said smilingly, "You are going to be my best disciple. I will teach you everything I know. I will learn new things so that I can teach you."

Disappointed, Jivaka said, "I thought you know everything"

Kashyapa said, "No one knows everything. If someone thinks so, they are fools. There is so much knowledge in the world that one human brain can only grasp some of it. Life is for continual learning. I hope you will learn that every day there is new learning. There is no end to learning."

Little Jivaka pondered over it, with his shoulders stooped, head bent!

Kashyapa laughed aloud and lifted him. "Some learning, in fact, most learning can be fun. I will teach you how to play chess but only after you eat something." By that time, one of the disciples had arrived and was cooking something. Jivaka's eyes lit up when he saw the beautiful chessboard with finely carved white and black kings, queens, knights, castles, horses and pawns.

By late morning, the mothers with sick children started arriving. Kashyapa spent the time examining the sick children and asking the mothers for details of the symptoms. He called his disciples who were arriving one by one, to prepare the decoctions and pastes, prepare poultice, decoctions to drink and dispensed them to the mothers, reassuring them that the child would recover soon if they followed the instructions.

Jivaka sat next to him, watching all the happenings, mesmerised by all the activity. The clients and disciples alike were surprised to see a small child sitting next to the sage. But no one dared to ask the sage whose child he was. Soon enough, he was a fixture in the ashram. Only the old man in Richika's ashram had an idea who he could be. But he was the one who would carry the secret to his death.

After the patients went away, Kashyapa, Jivaka and the disciples sat together and had a simple yet delicious meal of 'sali' rice and dal, along with thick buttermilk churned fresh as usual.

In the afternoon, Kashyapa left Jivaka to amuse himself, talking to the disciples or playing outdoors. A couple of disciples not yet twelve years of age, in fact, preferred to play for hours after the older disciples left for home.

The first night, Kashyapa asked, "Do you want me to tell you a story?"

Jivaka said, "I know lots of stories. I can also make new stories myself. But can you please tell me about the patients you saw in the morning. Please tell me what were the problems, what caused them and how you treated them!"

This request was met with stunned silence from Kashyapa. He wondered who this child was, who was so sophisticated in his talk despite being brought up by a washerwoman.

Kashyapa said, "I think I can try, but I need to know what you have already understood."

Pondering, Jivaka said, "The first child who was brought here was about one-year-old and was crying a lot, touching his ears. He was wrapped warmly in lots of clothes, his mother was crying too because he was hot to touch and was not sleeping."

Kashyapa said, "Sometime children get ear ache and have fevers. Then they cry, lose appetite and sleep poorly. I gave ear drops made of garlic, told the mother how to cool his body. But most important is not to worry—as this is very common in children. Adults in panic try all sorts of remedies and make it worse."

Jivaka said, "And the next one was..."

Kashyapa was surprised as he described all the twelve cases to little Jivaka, who heard him with rapt attention. It was indeed astonishing that Jivaka had noticed special aspects he himself, the royal paediatrician, had failed to notice. He said to himself, "This child is going to be my teacher!"

Jivaka, having had a long, extraordinary day, fell asleep sitting in front of Kashyapa. Kashyapa gently lifted him, put him in his bed on a wooden bench. He then pulled another wooden bench, rolled out a mattress and made his own bed. Before sleeping, he thought of the extraordinary day that brought him this precocious disciple. He had despaired of finding one as he was approaching his fifties.

At four in the morning, as he woke up, he found Jivaka too sitting up and rubbing his eyes. Kashyapa ruffled Jivaka's hair and said, "The dawn is two hours away, you can sleep till the sunrise."

Groggily, Jivaka said, "But I too want to come with you, bathe in the Ganga and meditate."

Kashyapa said, "You can swim and bathe and play on the sand. Meditation is for old people like me!"

"Oh," said Jivaka, "All right, I will play and swim when you meditate! But what do you meditate for?"

Kashyapa was lost for words. Finally, he said, "You can meditate, taking the name of the Gods, or you can meditate thinking of nothing, keeping your mind calm!"

Jivaka said, "Oh, but I like to think. I don't think I will ever meditate!"

Kashyapa said, "You are wise. Go and play!"

When Kashyapa opened his eyes at sunrise, he saw Jivaka, a moving silhouette against the glorious orange sky tinted with red, touched by pink clouds. When they went close, Kashyapa found Jivaka totally absorbed. Jivaka looked up and said, "Tata, how do you like my castle and kingdom?" Using wet sand, pebbles, rocks, driftwood and sticks, Jivaka had indeed built a royal city.

Kashyapa said, "I am impressed. I don't think I can make anything so beautiful. Have you seen a big city?"

"No, but I have heard about it in stories, that Tata at Ganga temple had told me!"

Kashyapa said "Can you tell me about the city?"

Jivaka said, "I call it Jivakapur. It is part of a kingdom given to Jivaka, the physician by the grateful king, when Jivaka saved his only son, the prince from death by healing him!" He looked up and smiled.

Kashyapa's eyes misted. "You want to be a healer, Jivaka? Healer of children?"

"Yes, Tata, Yes. I want to do what you do. Bring joy to all those mothers and their children. Will you take me as your disciple? When you do, I will address you as the Master not Tata."

Kashyapa said, "I am glad that I have a three-year-old disciple who has a long life ahead to learn and learn." He continued, "But I will formally accept you as a disciple after the *Upanayana* ceremony after you are five years old! I know you can recite shlokas like an expert. But three years is too young to be a disciple."

"But can I learn from you every night, as you told me

last night! It was so interesting—better than *Ramayana* and *Mahabharata* stories—because these are real."

"Of course. I will teach you everything but I don't want others to say that I have taken a baby as a disciple."

Before Jivaka could interrupt, Kashyapa said "I know you are not a baby—when it comes to intelligence and knowledge—but you do look like a small child!"

Jivaka said, "But...But...I have a question. Don't you think one child can understand another child better? Feeling for the other person is important to a physician. So a child physician is more suited to treat a child—if he has the knowledge. I think a lady physician is better for women patients and a man physician is better for treating men!"

Kashyapa was amazed. "I believe you are right!"

Jivaka jumped up and down and shouted, "I am Jivaka, disciple of the great Sage Kashyapa!"

Kashyapa smiled...

The Present

The Dream That Is A Nightmare

It was freezing cold. I could see a range of green mountains beyond which lie the snow mountains. Both shared the reflected grandeur of the rising sun. The river flowed majestically, yet very slowly under the icy sheet of frozen water on the top. I was shivering in awe at the cold beauty of the river. It must be the Ganga. No other river can hold you spellbound. As I was standing, I saw a tiny figure moving towards the river. I tried to call out. He was too small to be out there alone. I tried to call but my voice failed as if it was too frozen to come out. I could hear voices of adults in the background, behind me, but as in the case of nightmares, one could not will one's body to obey, I could not turn around to look! Clamour of voices, "Yes! Yes! Yes!" I heard a male voice that said, "No child, No. You don't have to do it. No—No—No!" The boy, smilingly, turned towards the voice, then walked away but in a most respectful manner and then ran away to jump into the river.... Soon his head went under water. The head full of black shiny ringlets was no longer to be seen. I screamed silently cursing my paralysed body!

When the phone shrilled, I woke up with a start, I was cold and clammy. Happy that it was only a nightmare. I had not really let a child die. I said, "Hello?"

"I am sorry doctor, calling you so late, especially when you are not on call," Sister Kanta said apologetically. I shook my head, happy that I could move and speak.

"That is okay. What is the problem?"

Sister Kanta said, "I did something terribly wrong officially, but I am sure you would support it."

I was impatient. "What is it? Tell me."

Sister Kanta said, "At 8 O'clock at night, a pregnant woman turned up in the hospital. She alighted from an auto rickshaw all alone. She was already having contractions in rapid succession. We put her on a stretcher and wheeled her to the operation theatre. The doctor on duty attended to her. If I had waited for formalities of paperwork and, especially in view of the rule about never admitting someone without an attendant, she would have delivered the baby on the hospital steps." She paused and almost whispered, "And she could have died."

I was alert and completely awake. “Sister Kanta, what has happened?”

Sister Kanta said, “Doctor, the mother is dying, the baby is alive. What do we do? We have no identification of the woman. She came in with nothing.”

I took a deep breath and said, “Okay, I will come straight away.”

Sister Kanta said, “You are my God. Thank you.” She was terrified of the consequences of her reckless admission of an unidentifiable woman and an infant soon to be motherless.

I got ready and rushed into the operation theatre. I glanced at the baby—apparently healthy, in a neonate's cubicle. Sister Kanta looked up at me and whispered, “She is sinking.” The young woman was bleeding badly. The drips did not seem to be doing anything. She was pale but her eyes focused on me. I had to go to her. With sudden strength, she snatched my hand, held it tight and said, “Keep my baby. He is precious. Take care of him.”

I soothingly placated her, “Yes, yes.” I did not know what else to say to the dying woman. Was it the time to explain that I am an unmarried woman wedded to the profession—a workaholic with no time for herself—let alone for a baby? Then the woman was no more. The gynaecologist on duty, my friend Vimla said, “What a mess, the body goes to the mortuary and then, we file a police report about the unknown woman. But what do we do about the baby? We will call the orphanage.”

I said, “Okay. But anyway, I will check if the infant is okay.”

I went to the cubicle and stood at the door and looked at the little fellow. It was wondrous. He was only 20-30 minutes old. His head was full of curly black ringlets. He was craning his head and looking at the bright lights. Can you believe it? He was just a newborn. Dark large eyes were already focusing and looking at the lights! Usually, you find them dopey or crying. But this one was amazing. Then he looked at me! I could not believe it. I went to him, his eyes tracked me. As I started examining him, he held my fingers tight!

Sister Kanta said, "Is it not amazing, he is not like a newborn at all. He is so alert. Poor thing, poor, poor thing already an orphan." Then she said speculatively, "Doctor—orphanages do not do a good job of taking care of newborns. They mostly die. Sometimes the hospital lets us keep the baby for a while before sending them to the orphanage, so that their feeding and sleep schedules are settled. Anyway, we have to start the paperwork, on that, the poor mite!" She sighed.

I was back in my nightmare that moment. The child with black ringlets on the head and big eyes was drowning while I stood paralysed. Was it an omen? A portent that I had to save this child? Suddenly I knew I had to keep this baby and bring him up. I had promised a mother on her deathbed. I said, "Yes, but I will take him for a short time—settle him to a routine."

Sister Kanta was flabbergasted. "Doctor! You do not have to do that. It is my fault. I will get other nurses to help me and send him to the orphanage when he is ready!"

Then I asked Sister Kanta, "Is there anything that the

mother had, that I can keep for him?" Sister Kanta said "She had nothing on her. It is very strange but she had absolutely nothing. But she has the same birthmark on her left shoulder, as this baby has." She touched the birthmark, the only visible link between the dead mother and the poor infant. My heart melted. I took him in my arms and cuddled him and he snuggled cosily. Sister Kanta was looking at me strangely. It must seem odd, a paediatrician snuggling a baby! I told her, "Sister Kanta, please keep him here for the night. Tomorrow I will make arrangements to take him home."

Sister Kanta said, "You have not thought it through. You are impractical. You don't know how difficult it is to take care of a baby. Who will take care of him when you are on duty all hours of the day and night?"

My brain was racing. "I will ask my mother."

"She is old," Kanta said.

"But she is fit. She will understand."

"I am sure she will say: if you want a baby, get married and have one!"

I wondered. Only my mother could answer that. "Okay. I will ask her and then decide."

"That is better. You are being too impulsive and impractical, if I may say so, doctor!" She was stretching out her arms to take him. When I pressed my lips to his silken head, I did not want to leave him even for one night.

The rest of the night, I tossed and turned and early morning called my mother. She had been living alone in a big bungalow after my father's death some years earlier, refusing to move into my flat. "Mother, can I come and see you? It is urgent." She said, "Of course, come and have breakfast with me." Anytime with my mother was meal-time.

The moment she saw me, she knew that something serious was up. I started with my nightmare, soon the entire story of the new man in my life followed. She listened quietly, not interrupting. Not a word of admonition. At the end, I waited with bated breath. She simply hugged me and said, "Of course, you must keep him. He is a divine child: When you are at work, leave him with me."

My eyes filled with tears. I knew how much she loved her freedom. But this baby was ours! "Can I keep him forever?" "Of course," she said.

When I brought home the infant, my mother was already there. She was delighted. "What a beautiful baby. Look at him looking at me. Such long hair, like a one-year-old! See how he is grabbing my fingers. What are we going to call him?"

I said "Jivaka", surprising even myself. My mother said "What?" I said "Jivaka."

"It is nice. But where would you get a name like that?"

I said, "I was describing to you my nightmare. A bit of it was forgotten but it came back to me just now, when you asked about his name. In the dream, as I stood paralysed and speechless, as the child was walking into the Ganga, a lone voice was calling out 'No! No! No!' It was actually "No—Jivaka—No. No. Jivaka...No."

We both thought it was a nice name. Maybe it meant life force, or life energy! So Jivaka came home to us. I must sometime trace back and find the origins of this unusual name.

One Who Seizes Babies

If it had not been for an earlier commitment, I would not have gone on this trip, leaving Jivaka with my mother. I had already decided to cut down on unnecessary work.

I was supposed to leave my clinic at 4 O'clock in the evening. My taxi had arrived exactly at four. Unfortunately, I could finish seeing the last of the children only by 6 pm. I had brought my small overnight bag to the clinic to save time. As I was going to address a group of doctors in Shimoga on common childhood health problems, I had no need to carry my black medical bag. My session was slated for 12 noon next day. So arriving late did not really matter. I walked up to my taxi.

I was disappointed. It was an Ambassador car. My old travel agent was usually very capable and sent only the good cars. But I remembered my own special instruction. "I am going to travel on the rural roads. Send me a good and reliable driver who knows the area." I had planned several trips around the town. The driver seemed pleasant and competent. It turned out that it was his own car and so I did not dare criticise it. I asked him, "Is it too late to start? What will happen, if the car has a breakdown?" He said "Don't worry, there is nothing in this car which I cannot put right. Most of the night buses ply on this road even blindfolded. Even I have done this journey a hundred times in five hours!"

That seemed reassuring enough. I told the driver, "You can stop the car whenever you want tea." I had a morbid fear of drivers falling asleep on the wheels! I added, "…and also any decent place where we can have some snack or a meal."

I had had a long day. I leaned back and dozed off. I hardly noticed the dense traffic as we left Bangalore. We stopped for some coffee and hot idlis at a place where there were twenty buses but only one small restaurant with blaring music from Kannada movies. The car seemed to be losing speed and almost stopping several times. The driver, Ramachandra, was muttering. I asked, "What's the matter?" By now the drizzle earlier had become a heavy downpour. First he said, "Nothing." Then he said, "May be I need to stop and take a look at the engine. It is raining too heavily. May I please turn off a little further and take the car to a garage, which I know in a place close by."

We had no other option. I had sensed that the car had a major problem. It was safer to be in a shelter in such a downpour. Soon we turned off the main road, on to a mud road. Of course, all the roads looked muddy. At this point. I actually missed the fleet of night buses that went past you like whirlwind with blaring horns and flashing headlights. We must have gone very slowly for at least ten kilometres when Ramachandra discovered two things. One was that the engine of the car had ceased to purr and the other was that we were completely and totally lost. His face was ashen and his hands were trembling. He could sleep in the car till the morning. What was he to do with me? But I was a seasoned traveller whose travels were always jinxed. He was not to know that.

The silver lining was that the rains had completely stopped. In fact, there was moonlight. Ramachandra was so afraid and apologetic that I forgot I was the victim. I said, "Does not matter. We have to stop over here. Morning we can go to the main road and board a bus. Shimoga cannot be very far from here." We looked around and found some dim lights beyond. The village had areca nut gardens and banana plantations on the either side. The reflections of the moon could be seen on the areca palms and banana leaves.

We walked towards the light. Luckily for us, it was a tea stall. There was no electricity but a small kerosene lantern blazed, casting a golden light around. A shrivelled old man sat there chewing paan and relaxing. His jaws dropped suddenly when he saw us emerging out of the darkness. One could not say who was more scared, him or us!

Ramachandra explained the situation. The old man was a kindly man. He said, "You can stay here. I can make you some hot tea," and proceeded to make it on the earthen stove, re-lighting the cinders with dry firewood. As he started relaxing with his paan, he wondered, "How can I ask this lady, especially a doctor to sleep in this shack?"

I was afraid of being thrown out in the middle of the night. I said, "It is all right. Ramachandra can sleep here. I will sleep in the car!" The old man said, "No—No—that's not what I meant! There is a very famous Ayurvedic doctor who is also an astrologer. He is an old gentleman. He has this huge mansion. He lives alone with his cook and servants. He would not mind putting you up. He is an extraordinary doctor and a good man. In fact, he would like to meet a doctor. He has a lot of cattle, and even a bullock cart. He can reach you to the main road in the morning. All these areca nut gardens belong to him."

I wondered why, if he was so wealthy, he did not have a car. It would have been so convenient to borrow it and pay for it. By far, this was the best solution. The old man picked up his long torch and set about the task of taking us to the local physician. I glanced at my watch. It was about 10.30 at night.

We reached an old-fashioned bungalow. The large front veranda had huge and finely carved wooden pillars with gigantic rafters on them. The main door was half open, it had magnificent carving on the doors as well as the frame. It was more like an old palace than a house. I need not have worried about waking up the elderly physician. He was there on an easy chair, reading in the light of a bright lamp. It appeared as if he was quite used to late night visitors. He got up from the easy chair with great agility. He was a man in his eighties but sprightly and alert.

He took in the situation in a few seconds. He was such a gracious host. He called his cook and told her to arrange a bed for me and take me to have a wash. In about fifteen minutes before going to bed, I came out to thank the host. He had once again settled down to his reading. He looked up and smiled and said, "So you are a doctor. What is your specialty? Where are you going?" He was happy to hear that I was a paediatrician going to an Indian Medical Association meeting in Shimoga. He seemed to be a well-read Ayurvedic physician with good grounding in English. His English was rusty but Kannada was poetic. I could see large number of volumes of books on Ayurveda, in Kannada, Sanskrit and English along with novels in Kannada and English.

It seemed such a waste of time to go to sleep in the presence of such an interesting man. Ayurveda was something I had paid scant attention to in my years as a student and later as a practitioner. He said, "You know, I also practice children's medicine. It is called *Kumarabhrtya*! I am particularly interested in children's diseases, especially serious ones!" For once, I could not believe my ears. Here, in the remote village, where the people lived as they did thousands of years ago, the practice of medicine goes even beyond that. Here was this elderly gentleman who talked to me about children's diseases! With the natural arrogance of an allopathic specialist I said, "Are there Ayurvedic schools specialising in children's diseases? I cannot believe it!"

Pandit Jois smiled and said, "It must be there. Otherwise I would not have spent my lifetime studying and practising it."

I asked, "What is the proof that it works?" He said humbly, "I don't know whether my treatment works or it is all God's grace—but the children get better!" He said, "You know something, I have recently come across a reference which compares some of the disorders mentioned in Ayurveda and modern medicine. I have been dying to talk to some one about it. May be you were sent here for that purpose?"

I agreed very politely. I was sure it was all rubbish but I could not dream of insulting such a gracious gentleman. He seemed to have sensed my hesitancy intuitively. He added, "It is just an old man's rambling...forget it!"

The night was interrupted by the arrival of another set of shining flashlights. A young couple arrived with an infant in arms. It was wrapped up in old, torn cloths. Apparently they were from a very poor family. The young mother was well wrapped and supported by the husband. He was holding the infant.

Pandit Jois got up and asked the baby to be placed on the low wooden bench that was his examination couch. I regretted my action of travelling without my medical bag. Here I was in a situation as it would have been thousands of years ago. It dawned on me that most of the people in this country lived like this. Pandit Jois examined the baby thoroughly and wrapped him up again. He examined the mother and asked her questions about the baby and herself. He told her what diet to take and how to carry out fomentation for her breast abscess and what to do for the baby. He mixed some remedies for both of them, for the stomach and for fomentation. The way he spoke to the young parents, their panic faded away. They nodded happily and collected the medicine. The only time they appeared distressed was when they had to pay but had no money. Pandit Jois said, "With this big house and property, do you think I need money?" Then he laughed and said, "Ok, ok—I know you have the best jackfruit in your farm. Give me one when it is the season," and he winked. The young people went away. I was amazed. He, of course, did not need the money but he did not want them to feel it was charity either.

I said to him, "Please tell me: what you did and what did you give and what will happen?" Slowly and patiently, he described his treatment. "Of course, there is a difference in treatment of disorders in Ayurveda and modern medicine. I am, indeed, excited and would like to know more." I knew that I was in the presence of a great physician.

It was already 12 O'clock. Pandit Jois said, "I am an old man. I need my sleep. You also need to get up early. Maybe the discussion was not meant to be!"

I said, "Oh, no! I really want to spend some time with you. I need to learn from you. I can leave here at 10 o'clock in the morning and be in Shimoga on time."

I was up very early, at 4.30 in the morning. It must be all the excitement of the night. When I came out to the veranda after a wash, Pandit Jois was already there, working on some papers. He looked up and smiled and said, "This is as good a time as any! In fact, Brahma Muhurtam is the best time of day. Let us talk, but let me get you some coffee." His cook must have still been asleep. He brought coffee for both of us in gleaming bronze tumblers. He teasingly said, "I make the best coffee in the whole world." I took a sip and said, "I agree whole-heartedly."

Straightaway he plunged into a discourse, as if he knew the questions in my mind. "You see, there are around 48 common diseases of childhood. These are cough, cold, wheezing, fever, various aches, pain in the limbs, eye, ear, throat problems and so on. I am sure they are all there in the modern paediatric disorders. But what intrigues me is the group of serious and often fatal disorders. These are called '*Graha rogas*' which means these are caused by 'seizure' of the babies by the *grahas*. The word *graha* means that which seizes. I said, "Does *graha* not mean planets or signs of the zodiac?"

"Yes, generally. But not in Ayurvedic paediatrics. I will read you descriptions of twelve diseases, you tell me at the end of each description, your diagnosis in modern paediatrics."

I was amazed, "Really, let us try". I was sure it was all hocus-pocus.

Pandit Jois started. "For example, the child has inflammation of the eyes, deviation of the angle of the mouth, refuses to suckle, closes the eye, does not cry much and has tightened fists. He is constipated and emits smell of blood. What is your diagnosis?" Taken aback by the description, I said, "Facial palsy."

He said, "Now the next one: The child has excessive tears, from one eye, half side of the body is paralysed, has recurrent convulsions, body becomes stiff and there is drooping of the neck. The child sweats excessively. He appears frightened, restless and bites his lips. There is a deviation of the mouth, excessive salvation. There is involuntary movement of one eye, eyebrow and face. He holds his fist tight and has flushing of face. He is also constipated. What is your diagnosis?"

"Polio encephalitis."

"Now the third one: There is recurrent loss of consciousness, with irregular movements of limbs with frothing in the mouth. Child may pull his own hair, bite his tongue or mother's nipples. Child may pass urine and stools involuntarily. There may be yawning or a typical cry or scream. This may be accompanied by fever and awakening in the night. The body smells like pus and blood. What is your diagnosis?"

"Epilepsy or seizures!"

"Now the next: There is stiffness of body, bending in the middle, loss of consciousness with irregular movements, limbs, clenching fists and biting of lips and appears fearful, upward deviation of eye, continuous fever. May be associated with hiccough, diarrhoea / vomiting and cough. There is swelling in one ear. The child emits the smell of goat!"

"It is truly amazing. The diagnosis is meningitis. What is

it with smells of illness?"

The cook came out at this juncture and called us for breakfast. I was unwilling to break the conversation. Pandit Jois said smilingly. "These are not real patients. It is only a clinical description. Come, let's have breakfast."

There was a sumptuous breakfast of freshly steamed rice vermicelli, with delicious coconut chutney and coconut milk sweetened with jaggery. The coffee was grown in his own yard. So were the coconuts and the rice. It was a homely breakfast. I said, "I would die for this breakfast." The cook was pleased. The remarkable gentleman said, "That is specially made for special visitors. Poor me. I get only idlis." The cook laughed aloud. "You are the one to tell me what to make! Why don't you ask for rice vermicelli everyday?"

We resumed our conversation.

"The child has tremors, sweating, closing of eyelids, and erection of body hair. He may bite his tongue. Posture is episthotonos, he has a strange cry or bark like dog. Runs around and emits faecal smell."

I am amazed. "Rabies!"

"Now child passes loose stools of green colour or of different colours. The abdomen has nodules or prominent veins occur over the abdomen. The child gradually becomes emaciated. Associated features are, falling of hair, aversion to food, weak voice, discolouration of skin and cries excessively. The child emits the smell of eagle."

I was most impressed. "It is Koch's Abdomen—but only

we don't add the smell of eagle to the description. Perhaps we should!"

"The last one of the twelve. The child has altered appetite, abdomen has blackish, bluish veins. The child looks dull. Hand, feet of the child appear beautiful. Looks irritable and may suffer from fever. The child may smell of urine."

I said, "It is unbelievable—but correct. It is the Indian childhood cirrhosis. It is amazing and you say these descriptions were documented more than a thousand years ago."

"It is truly amazing." I say. He says, "Only problem is that we have definite names for these disorders. These are based on demonology. These were truly demons for children. As no one knew the causes, these were attributed to demons who seize the babies."

I asked, "What about the treatments?"

"There are many herbs, ointments, fomentation, fumigation and also rituals. This is what I want to know: whether these can be tested scientifically. I only know the healing properties of the system by experience, but I want to be able to convince you."

"I could not but agree," I said.

Then he added in jest, "You know there are twelve *grahas*. Five are males and seven are females. There are descriptions of these *grahas* as there are of Gods in the Hindu pantheon."

For example, the chief of the *grahas* is Skanda. He has been described as wearing golden crown, attired in red and wearing a garland of red flowers. His body is covered with sandal paste and he has a charming personality. Revathi is a female *graha* who is dark complexioned and wears attires of different colours. Her body is covered with sandalwood paste. She wears dangling earrings!"

I mentally vowed to return one day to study in detail treatments for babies who are seized by the *grahas*. As he bade goodbye, Pandit Jois said, "Have a safe journey. And say good bye to me like the local people by saying 'I will come' and not 'I will go'."

Saying "I will come," I waved to him, then changed my mind, walked back and touched his feet before I left. I had never done this in my life!

Dreams And Memories

It is Jivaka's third birthday. I am sitting with my mother and watching Jivaka, the joy of our lives, playing by himself, putting together a jigsaw with a thousand pieces! This child is truly amazing. This is what he wanted on his birthday. He said he was tired of all those baby jigsaws.

Mother said, "Vatsayani, it is truly amazing what this child has brought to our lives. Is it not?", thinking that he was so absorbed he could not hear them. He looked up and smilingly said, "Thank you, Grandma!"

I looked at my mother and she at me—amazed. I said, "If we want to keep something a secret we need to go far away.

Probably he would hear what we say and even know what we think! Right, Jivaka?"

He said, "I don't think I can hear you if you are in the next room. But it is very rarely that I get to know what you think."

We both burst into laughter. At that moment, the child next door, Vatsa, Jivaka's friend, called him out to play. He left the jigsaw saying, "Please don't move it, I have not completed it," and went away. I looked at my mother and said, "Mother, I had that dream again. Sometimes I wonder about rebirth. I have told you only about the dream I had the night Jivaka was born. That is a recurrent dream. But occasionally, I get other dreams too—very vivid—definitely belonging to the olden days, perhaps even centuries before…"

She said, "Yes?"

"After we brought Jivaka home, I had a dream in which I saw a very beautiful young woman, may be about 15 years old, holding an oil wick lamp, and going and virtually seducing a rishi in his thirties. I thought it was very strange. It did not appear unclean or obscene. It was beautifully romantic. All I could hear was her saying, 'I want your son'!"

"How very strange!", mother said.

"The next dream came a few months later. This was even stranger. It was almost exactly like the night Jivaka was born. The woman delivering the baby was the same young woman I saw some months before, wanting the son of the Rishi. Her face was pale, anaemic, full of pain, yet stoic and serene. Even as the dream ended midway, I knew that she died at childbirth."

Somehow, I felt this is what happened. The recurrent dream is probably when the baby was five years old.

Jivaka came back with Vatsa and some other friends. He said to me, "We want you to come out to see our drama."

Jivaka was the youngest, yet he had organised a play. A play about Krishna and his mischief. The dialogues, the songs and dances were simply enchanting. By the time the drama ended, the whole neighbourhood had collected and burst into applause.

This child of mine is unusually talented. There was nothing he did not find interesting. He was already reading, by simply listening and looking at the stories I was reading to him at night before bedtime.

He asked me and my mother questions that we could not answer, forcing us to look up encyclopaedias. When I picked up this baby in the hospital, I had no premonition that I was bringing home a prodigy and a genius. Now it is my job to see he gets a normal and healthy childhood. He is such a happy child that it is no chore at all to take care of him.

Sometimes, I am worried when I find him totally preoccupied. When I ask him what he is thinking, he says, "This is my other world!" I ask him, "Who is in that world? Am I there?" he says seriously, "It is a very old world—people dress differently, speak differently, there are good and bad people—but mostly good. I have not seen you there so far!"

I do get worried. Does Jivaka have a problem? I know that young children have imaginary playmates. But imaginary world? Perhaps he will outgrow it sometime. I think, he knows about my worry. Nowadays he talks less and less about the other world. Perhaps if I am not so worried, he may confide in me but I cannot but worry. After all he is only three. How can he create a parallel world?

But preoccupation or day-dreaming never interferes with what he is doing here and now. It merges seamlessly with whatever he does.

In the pre-school, they tell me that they want him to be placed in the higher grade as he excels in everything. I don't know if it is good for him.

I go to sleep worrying about the decision. I have a dream, a very vivid dream. I am in an ashram in Haridwar. I am sitting at the feet of a sanyasi dressed in white. He smiles and tells me, "Don't worry, Jivaka will cope with everything. Nothing is a burden on him. He carries with him ancient *samskaras*. These protect him."

I wake up, at peace and happy. I tell my mother, "In my dream the sanyasi in the ashram said to me, 'My child, a banyan tree does not need any shelter. It is the duty of the tree to shelter the whole world.' Sometimes I have worried why this child is so independent."

Mother said, "I too have wondered about this divine child."

I was astonished "Why would you call Jivaka the divine child? You did it when he came to us the first time."

Mother said "I don't know really. I simply said it, yet it is true, is it not?"

Mother said, "Vatsayani, I too have had dreams, but I paid no attention to them—because they were so strange and meaningless. They are fleeting dreams, unconnected sequences —for example, a very young man carrying one old man in a wicker basket on his back and helping another one with a stick and climbing mountains, by the looks of it the Himalaya! Whatever could it be?"

I confessed that I too did not know what it meant.

She added, "Another time I saw a group of sanyasis interrogating a small child in a very aggressive manner, yet the child staying calm and respectful."

Jivaka came, in finishing all his games, looked up and said to us, "Discussing dreams?"

"How do you know?"

"I too have them."

I asked, "What do you dream?"

"Oh, this and that…all fun!"

But he suddenly became serious and said, "Dreams and memories connect the past, the present and the future!"

I and my mother exclaimed together, "What?"

Jivaka said, "Nothing, Just some silly joke I heard on TV."

Jivaka's Birthday

Vatsayani had taken a day off to celebrate Jivaka's fifth birthday. First thing she did was to call her mother and to reminisce on the oddest event in their lives, namely the arrival of Jivaka. They both loved him so much. Sometimes Vatsayani's mother even wondered if she had enjoyed anything other than the time spent with Jivaka. What an amazing, yet impulsive decision they had both made. Never a dull moment with Jivaka around: always talking, laughing and loving, all the time they had known him. Not a day's illness, not a whimper, not a sulk. Amazing indeed.

Mother said, "Give him a hug and kiss and birthday

greetings. I will be coming around shortly to help with the party."

Vatsayani softly went into Jivaka's room, sat on the chair waiting for him to wake up. He was asleep, with smile on his face: probably dreaming of his party, Vatsayani thought.

At the sight of that lovely face and tousled black curls, Vatsayani's eyes misted. She said, "My child—my own child—what a treasure." Not once did the thought occur that she was still single. She had numerous friends, men and women. Men she kept at arm's length, no one could love Jivaka as much as she did. She could never share him with anyone. She knew her mother worried about her, wanted her to have a family of her own. Often she said, "I will keep Jivaka and take care of him—please find a husband for yourself." The firm answer was "No."

Jivaka moved slightly, opened his eyes, saw her, jumped up and came to cuddle her. "Mama!" Vatsayani said, "Happy birthday, Jivaka, from me and Grandma!"

"Oh! What have you got for me?"

"What you always wanted!"

"Bicycle?"

"Yes."

"Oh, where is it?" He ran to look for it. She was sure he would learn to ride it within a day. A gifted child he was. At three he could read, do puzzles with a hundred pieces and speak three languages, all of them fluently. He was playful, always up to some mischief, yet quite a serious little learner. She even wondered whether he was a genius: very precocious for his age. She never pushed him to learn anything; but there he was wanting to do millions of things.

He came back to her on his bike, slowly, with the supporting side wheels. "I want these off now!" He declared. Vatsayani had guessed he would say that.

The party was fun, eatables, toys and boys and girls to play. Jivaka shared all the gifts with his friends. Some of Vatsayani's friends too had come. They were sitting and enjoying the special treats Grandma had made for them, wondering at Vatsayani's inexhaustible energy in keeping the children entertained.

Finally, one by one, the children were collected by their parents. Jivaka was still bursting with energy. Grandma said, "Time for bath and bed!" and off they went. In the bath, Jivaka said, "Grandma, I think, Mama should get married to that good looking doctor who sat on the blue sofa and kept looking at her!"

Grandma was aghast! "What? I know he is a good friend and she likes him too!"

"I like him too. He does not fuss over me like the others do—but I like the way he talks to me—like a friend."

Grandma said, "You are too small. That's why you should not talk about, grown-ups like that!"

Jivaka said "Grandma, I love you both very much: but you are old, when I am grown up and go away, Mama will be alone. I don't like that."

Grandma knew that this little man was someone she could

honestly talk to. She said, "Mama is afraid that a man in her life will come between you and her."

Jivaka: "That may have been so all these years. But now I am growing up, I understand things better. I will not be jealous if Mama shares her love with someone else!"

Grandma said, "I really don't know what to say, Jivaka. I too wish she would get married."

Vatsayani walked in, having said goodbye to the guests and said, "Who is getting married?"

Jivaka said, "You!"

Vatsayani said, "What?"

Jivaka said, "Mama, I am big now, I want you to get married!"

Both Vatsayani and her mother fell silent and got him ready for bed.

The issue was not discussed again, but Vatsayani's mother did tell her what had transpired before her arrival in the bathroom.

Vatsayani: "Sometimes, it is scary the way he talks like an adult. How could he have such maturity at the age of five?"

Grandma said, "He is a divine child—that is how."

Vatsayani had a suitor, an eminently eligible colleague whom she liked immensely. For the last five years he had been proposing to her and getting a no for an answer. Jivaka was the reason. The seed of doubt that Jivaka planted on his birthday slowly led to the re-examination of her decision. A week after the birthday, Dr Vasanth came to her and said, "I must talk to you in private." They went out for a coffee. He said, "Vatsayani, I have tried my best to persuade you to marry me because I love you. But you have refused. I find it very hard to be around you when you are so emotionally distant from me. I am taking a transfer and going away. But remember, I will never love anyone. So I will always be waiting for you. You just have to give me the word."

Vatsayani said, "I will give the word now!"

"What?"

She smiled and said, "Jivaka says you love me and I too love you and we should get married!"

Next day Vatsayani took Jivaka out for an early dinner with Vasanth. Jivaka's future was her main concern. As they talked over dinner, Vasanth slowly broached the subject of marrying his mother. Jivaka said excitedly, "How many children have the good fortune of witnessing their mother's marriage!" Vasanth pursued, "How true. But when a small brother or sister arrives would you be upset?"

Jivaka said, "Why should I get upset? I would love to have lots of brothers and sisters!" Vatsayani was aghast. Vasanth shook with laughter saying, "That indeed is a tall order!"

Then Jivaka fell into a reverie as Vatsayani and Vasanth watched him closely.

Jivaka said, "Once upon a time, hundreds of years ago, I had many brothers and sisters. They all loved me and I loved them too. My mother was not my birth mother, my father was not my real father. But both of them loved me more than their own children. My birth mother died giving birth to me…"

"What?" Vatsayani and Vasanth simultaneously looked alarmed! The child knew he was adopted at birth, but this was too much. Then he looked up at them and smiled. "You know how I love making up stories!" Vatsayani let out a sigh of relief, she laughed. "I love your stories."

Vasanth asked, "Besides being a 'story maker', what would you like to be when you grow up?"

Jivaka ponderingly began, "Oh! A painter: I love painting. A musician: I love music. Traveller: I want to be an adventurer, travelling all over the world. But most of all—I want to be a pae…di…atri…cian—a doctor of children like both of you."

That put an end to all the questions Vasanth had sought.

"A healer of children!" Jivaka added.

The Black Holes In History

The Jivaka growing up centuries later had vague memories of the other Vriddha Jivaka. As he sat in his grade one classroom, he often remembered events that he was not sure he had witnessed. He remembered sitting by the side of his Master in an ancient land, learning. Sound of the waves of the river, the trees swaying in the scented breeze, trees laden with fruits—working on earth, growing plants. It was as if these belonged to another life. Perhaps he dreamt them. Those were exciting times.

The teacher called out, "Jivaka, can you multiply what is on the board?" Jivaka came out of his reverie and went to the board and completed the task—as ever correctly. The teacher wondered, "He looked so preoccupied but he is quite correct. Strange!" She thought she would catch him doing badly at least once. Amazing, this child! Perhaps he was dreaming about the holiday for which his mother was planning to take him. For a foster mother, she was better than most mothers with their own children.

Jivaka was his joyful self as they set out on a holiday. Vatsayani said, "We are going to Kashmir and you will see the snow for the first time."

"I have seen the snow—in the mountains!"

She laughed, "How could you? You may have seen it on TV or in your dreams."

He said "Perhaps" and did not persist as he normally did.

He asked, "Mother, have you ever had dreams that are real?"

"How can a dream be real?"

"But tell me have you ever had dreams about me?"

Vatsayani thought over it, how could she not remember her most fearful nightmare! She said, "Several times I have a recurring dream. It occurred for the first time the night you were born!"

"What is it?" He asked excitedly.

"It was about a child. Almost your age but dressed differently in loose white clothes, running to a frozen river, while an old man dressed similarly crying out running after the child saying 'No, no, no, Jivaka'. I don't know what happens, because every time the dream ends there. And I wake up with my heart beating fast. I feel as helpless as the old man. We don't know whether the child is alive or dead."

"Is that why you named me Jivaka?"

"Yes, indeed, and it is such a beautiful name."

"I too wonder how the story ended."

They both let the matter rest after that!

When Jivaka was twentyone, finally Vatsayani found the secret of her nightmare about Jivaka. She had come across this Ayurvedic tome. She skyped Jivaka. Jivaka, now in his twenties, was already on the way to becoming a paediatrician in an accelerated programme topping all the examinations he faced in the USA. Skyping was done when he wanted to see his brother and sister whom he loved dearly. But Jivaka had a separate place in her heart, no matter how dearly she loved her own family.

Jivaka was just up and was delighted to see her, wishing him happy birthday. No—that was not it—the rest of the family was not there. She was excited! Very excited. "Jivaka, guess what I found out about my nightmare. It was not a nightmare at all! It was a parent's nightmare of thousands of years—of one's child coming to harm. I found the book, the *Kashyapa Samhita*, alternately called..."

Jivaka completed the sentence and said, "*Vriddha Jivakiya Tantra*" and smiled.

Five Hundred Years Ago

Sometime between Vriddha Jivaka and the present-day Jivaka, five hundred years earlier, another child was growing up around Kanakhala. He was a descendant of Vriddha Jivaka, the famed healer of children. His name was Vatsya. His teacher believed that the child Vatsya was indeed a reincarnation of Jivaka. He too was a child prodigy. His teacher was a physician but Vatsya had decided that he wanted to be a paediatrician. The teacher was helpless. He said to the boy, "Much as I would like to help you—your ancestor Vriddha Jivaka had left his treatise *Kashyapa Samhita* at the Royal Court of Manjupattan—where he was invited by the Royal Physicians and they had no paediatricians among them. The King had no children as even the ones born died very young."

"But did he not return to the ashram of Kashayapa that he would have inherited?"

"The story is that he came back with a beautiful bride but without the tome, *Kashyapa Samhita*."

"So it must be in the Royal Court of Manjupattan. When I am older, I will find it. I owe it to my country and people and my forefathers that I find it and put it together again."

"But you are only five-years-old, my child."

"But Jivaka was only five when he was anointed Vriddha Jivaka! I have to bring back his treatise to our country!"

The master only nodded his head.

If the child were even half a genius as Vriddha Jivaka was, he would probably succeed in his quest.

"Master, do you know why *Kashyapa Samhita* has two names—*Kashyapa Samhita* or *Vriddha Jivakiya Tantra*?"

"I do not know my child. In practice, *Samhitas* are compiled by the scribes but are not named after them!"

Vatsya lapsed into a dream state. He was absently rubbing the birthmark on his left shoulder, wondering about the mystery of the missing *Vriddha Jivakiya Tantra!*

The Past

Jivaka, The Disciple

Kashyapa made Jivaka sit next to him and said, "There are ten *samskaras* in childhood. I will describe them to you. In your life, some are in the past but I don't know if you had them or not. But I want you to have two of them now that are appropriate. These are tonsure and *Upanayana*. I have asked Sage Richika in the next ashram for help."

"If I have not had the earlier ones, why should I have them now?"

Kashyapa, "These are meant to set the life course that is right in motion. Your life earlier was set on course by good people around. Now it is my duty to perform these rituals.

This is the ritual part. But for me, as a physician these have even greater significance.

"Tonsure symbolises an entry into a new state beyond infancy. The physician can examine the head for closing of fontanel, and possible bumps suggestive of injuries, tumours, etc. The other day you, along with me, palpated the head of a baby. You saw for yourself how soft the top of the head was. But as the baby grows older it gets a head full of hair. I still need to examine him properly. However, tonsure has several symbolic meanings. Can you think of any, Jivaka, my child?"

"Oh, yes, it makes you ugly!"

Kashyapa laughed aloud. "You are right! Anything else?"

"When you are ugly—people make fun of you—humiliate you!"

Kashyapa said "Then?"

Jivaka nodded, "When people laugh at you—you know that it is only your hair that you lost—not your head. So you are who you are—with or without the trivial thing that makes you vain!"

Kashyapa was silent. Then he said, "You are right! So you have no problem about the tonsure!"

"No!" Jivaka said emphatically. "I want you to make sure my head is okay. I want to be a healer like you!"

Kashyapa, the healer of children, was so moved he drew Jivaka into a rare tight hug.

"The next ritual is *Upanayana*, where the guardian hands over the child to the guru as a disciple. Then onwards the disciple belongs to the Guru and not his family."

Jivaka laughed, "That is not a problem, as I don't have a family. I loved being with you. When I first came, I was afraid, I may not like it here. I would miss Yadu, my brothers and sisters, my parents and my Tata. But here I have so much to learn that I have no time. But I do remember them. When I am twelve I will go and see them. Is it all right?"

"Of course, you must make them happy for the trust they place in me to bring you up."

Much later, when Jivaka had started coming to Richika's ashram regularly, once Jivaka asked, "Why is Nachiketa so obsessed with who his father is?"

Richika looked up, now he could barely see the outlines of the little boy's face or figure.

"You don't think it is necessary?"

Jivaka said, "I don't ask who my father is. Back when I was a baby—Tata, was my father—now Sage Kashyapa and you are my fathers. It does not matter who the real parents are. Those who take care of you and teach you are the mother, father and the Guru. They are all the same!"

Richika did not have anything more to say.

Who was this child—where did he come from? He recalled the sequence of events that had occurred when this little one came to Kashyapa's ashram.

Once he had asked Ramananda, "By the way, where is

the young woman you got rid of in a huff for speaking in the presence of scholars?"

The old man was puzzled. "I don't know. I scolded her and sent her away for her impudence the day she interfered with your scholarly discussions."

"But she was right. Why did you send her away? She was useful at the ashram!"

The old man said, "She was not a girl of good character. I cannot have such character around here in your and Sage Kashyapa's ashram."

"Why do you say that?"

"Oh, just a thought. She was too bold and impudent despite being very useful around the ashram. I am glad she is gone. It is a huge responsibility to have a personable young woman around here."

"Any idea where she could have gone?"

Ramanada sat up, "Why do you want to know?"

Richika said, "I simply asked—idle curiosity!"

"Well, don't be curious. She is not worth it." That was the end of that discussion.

Then Ramananda had come up to Richika and waited silently as he pored over his palm leaf treatises. Richika looked up and said kindly, "What is the matter?"

Ramananda said, "Sage Kashyapa has a foundling!"

"What?"

"There is a small child in the ashram. Sage Kashyapa says that he was found on the banks of the Ganga the other day."

"How strange! But how can he keep the child? He has to give it away to someone to adopt."

"Why?" asked the old man.

"What do you mean? How can he take care of a child in the ashram?"

"He is a children's physician. Of course, he can! I know, you possibly cannot. But the sage can!" He chuckled as Richika brooded over this. Suddenly Richika was lost in the luminous vision of the young woman, who promised to bear his son and disappeared from his life.

Kashyapa, in one of rare forays outside his ashram, had come to Richika's door. Old man Ramananda ran out, paying obeisance and ushered him in. Richika said, "What an honour Sage Kashyapa! What brings you here? I just heard that you have adopted a child. What is it all about?"

Kashyapa said, "Yes, that is the reason why I am here. This foundling is only three-years-old but is a genius. So I am obliged to bring him up. My destiny! I suppose I want him to be my disciple and become a healer of children. But I need your help!"

"My help! I know nothing about children."

"Oh no, not about bringing him up. I can do that. He is a healthy good-natured child. It is about some of the rituals. I need someone to be notionally his guardian before he becomes my disciple."

"Why me?"

"You are my neighbour and I trust you. Also in the next

ten years you may need more help than what your old man can give," alluding to his failing eyesight, "this child will be a young man when we are older."

"That seems reasonable. What do you want me to do?"

"I need you to perform two rituals for this child. By the way, his name is Jivaka. I want you to do his tonsure, *Chudakarma*. It gives me a chance to examine his head and, shortly thereafter, his *Upanayana* and hand him over to me as his Guru."

"But I am not his parent!"

"It is only notional. I am not saying you are his parent. With the completion of these two rituals, I shall be relieved of the anxiety of not taking him as a disciple as per the rules laid down in the *Grhyasutras*."

"If you say so. I shall certainly do whatever you say. But I know nothing about these things."

"One more thing, I want you to allow him to sit around when scholars visit you, so that he learns more than what I can teach."

"But what will he do? He is only a baby!"

"You will be surprised. He is an exceptionally bright child!"

Kashyapa left with a smile on his face.

Ramananda muttered, "I wonder what was all that about?"

Richika said, "He is a very wise man—whatever he asks is something I will cherish and gladly do—even if I do not know or care about it. Why do you think it is odd?"

Ramananda said, "No. No. Nothing of the sort. The whole

thing is a rather curious affair!"

"Curious? Why? He found a child and he wants my help for some rituals. He has always been so helpful to me."

Ramananda was silent. Somewhere in the recesses of his mind he knew that the situation was just right. It was destined. He had a vague feeling that the child's face was familiar. But he could not ask Richika. Kashyapa could do no wrong.

After that, when he was barely four, Jivaka started coming regularly to sit with Richika as a minor disciple, when he had free time. He was an avid learner. Once, as Richika was trying hard to read an unusually illegible tiny script, Jivaka asked "Master, may I read it to you?"

"What? Can you read?"

Jivaka shyly nodded and reached for the palm leaf. He started reading flawlessly, with perfect diction. Richika was delighted. He was slowly going into depression as his vision was failing. Now this divine child offered to read to him. He wiped his tears of joy. A new birth. He could continue his pursuit of knowledge and truth because of Kashyapa's gift. The boy read on, learning the meaning with sentence, hardly aware of the joy on Richika's face. Somewhere in the labyrinths of his mind, Richika heard the soft voice, "Son of mine will be your eyes!"

He shook his head—thinking what an absurd thought!

Days passed as Richika once again delighted in his studies, with Jivaka not only being his eyes, but also an interlocutor. Sometimes one can learn so much from a mere child!

Ramananda was, in addition, worried about Richika's eyesight. It was deteriorating rather rapidly. He was himself getting on in age, may be Richika should get someone else to care for him. He had to wait for the right time to broach the subject—that perhaps he should get married. When he did it, Richika suddenly asked him, "What about that girl you brought to the ashram sometime back?"

"What?" said the astounded Ramananda.

"Why not, she was pretty and bright."

Richika said wistfully, "I would have married that girl whom you called impudent and had brought here, looking like a drowned rat."

"What about your celibate vows?"

"Oh, yes," Richika sighed. "You are right. Now that I am going blind, it would be terrible mistake to marry anyone."

That was the end of the conversation. It was a closed subject between the two, never to be brought up again. Some years later, when Richika was almost blind, the old man planned to bring his grandson to care for Richika.

Upanayana

Kashyapa called Jivaka and said, "Today is your birthday and we are going to have your Upanayana!"

Jivaka said "How do you know when my birthday is?"

Kashyapa; "Your mother told me when she gave me your horoscope and also it is an auspicious day, in Uttarayana under an auspicious star."

Jivaka asked, "What is this ceremony?"

Kashyapa gave details and instructed the disciples to do the various tasks.

"I am going to Sage Richika to invite him."

"Why?"

"Because you needed to be given away to me as part of the ritual. So he will stand in for your father—give you to me as a disciple."

"But even without ceremony I have been your disciple."

"Oh, please do it to make me happy."

"I will do anything to make you happy." Then Jivaka added, "So I have to address you as my guru and not Tata anymore!"

"That does not matter, you can address me the way you like."

"Oh, no. I must address you like all others do—people must not mistake it for lack of discipline."

Then Jivaka asked, "Can anybody have the *Upanayana*?"

"Oh yes, at different ages for other castes, slightly older than Brahmin boys. A Brahmin teacher can have disciples of all the other castes. But the reverse is not true."

"Can a shudra too be a disciple?"

"Yes, provided he is intelligent and comes from an enlightened family."

Jivaka says, "Yes, like my mother and her family and my brothers Yadu and others!"

The ceremony started: "Now is the time," pronounced Kashyapa giving Jivaka to Richika. Richika lifted Jivaka and said, "He is light as a feather! Surprising!"

On the ground, a bed for Lord Brahma was prepared for oblation, sanctifying *ghrta* (ghee) poured, and the sacrificial palsa wood dipped in ghee was lit.

Kashyapa uttered the words of the mantra 'Svaha' each for fire, air, Prajapathi, Kashyapa, Ashvinis, Indra, Danavanthri, Saraswathi, Purnbhaga and to much-worshipped Agni! Kashyapa was given the sacrificial pot of honey as he was to be the teacher.

Jivaka was given a bowl of curds to eat, facing the east and reciting the mantra of *Dhadikarana*; touching the water, going around the fire from the right side. Then he touched the hand of Kashyapa and said, "I am your son" and after touching his feet said, "I am your disciple."

Kashyapa, thanking Richika, led Jivaka away, explaining, "A physician is a thrice born: first the normal birth; then after the *Upanayana* the second one, after completion of the training for being a physician (Vaidya) the third birth. With all my blessings may you be a thrice born!"

Smiling at the memory of this child's first day with him after his arrival—his sand castle on the banks of the Ganga—Kashyapa mused.

The lessons began in earnest the next day, till then it had been all night-time stories. As Jivaka joined the other disciples and sat in front of Kashyapa in quiet obedience, Kashyapa described the qualities of a disciple.

"He should be forgiving, clever, dextrous, suitable, clean, born of good family, religious, truthful, non-violent, peaceful, knowledgeable with critical understanding, skilful and with zeal.

"He should have the habit of following instructions. He should be chaste and free from greed and envy."

Kashyapa added, but the teacher should have also certain qualities.

"He should be religious, possess knowledge, expert in reasoning and tactics, sober looking, clean and pure, well-wisher of the disciple, giver of instructions, expert in explanation of medical science, with full knowledge and critical understanding, auspicious, not doing any other work except teaching with qualities described."

He says to the disciples, "Further, you should be modest, favourable to me, religious, ascetic, always willing to study when called for, communicate everything to me and have knowledge of appropriateness of time and place. You should be endowed with fortitude and patience. You should avoid greed, anger, delusion, envy, frivolousness, animosity, wine, meat and women. After the service of the teacher, in the time left over, you should study. You should not practise medicine without the permission of the teacher, without reverence or without completion of the study."

The disciples silently nodded together in acceptance.

For once, Jivaka did not ask a question: he was practising implicit obedience.

Kashyapa continued, "Now with the method of study. All of you have been doing odd jobs around the ashram but not really given formal instruction. We start it today from the youngest to the eldest."

"Both alert students and the pious teacher should sit in an auspicious place, raise hands and say '*Om*' or '*atha*'. This should be followed by recitation of Savitri mantra three times. Then the teacher teaches one subject and repeats it. The student too repeats and memorises it. One should memorise the subject, tolerating contradictions and without pre-conceived notions. This should be followed by practising it and real knowledge of facts."

He continued,"While the above are the ideal conditions, there are times when one should not study. These are: during vacations, festivals, during ill-health of the teacher, Brahmin, cow, oneself or others. Or at twilight, lightning, meteor falls, rain without clouds, sun being invisible. One should not practise when hungry, thirsty, ill or mentally dejected. One should not study a subject not taught by the teacher. One should not read in too loud, protracted or slow and weak voice."

He added: "Today we start the lesson. What is Ayurveda? '*Ayu*' is life, '*vid*' denotes knowledge. The knowledge that promotes longevity or does not diminish longevity is Ayurveda. There are eight branches: Kumarabhrtya (Obstetrics, Gynaecology and Paediatrics). Kayachikitsa (Internal Medicine) Salya Hartrka (Surgery), Salyaka (Diseases of the Ear, Throat and Nose), Visatantra (Toxicology), Bhutatantra (Demonology) Agadatantra (Preventive Medicine) and Rasayanatantra (Rejuvenation). Ayurveda was created by Brahma for protection of all living beings of the universe. He gave it to Ashwins, they to Indra and Indra to the four sages Kashyapa, Vasistha, Atri and Bhrigu. They gave it to their sons and disciples. People of four castes can study it. Brahmana for knowledge and kindness to mankind, Kshatriya to protect the public, Vaishya for livelihood and Shudra to serve others."

He expanded: "As God Agni is foremost, Kumarabhrtya is the foremost among the eight branches.

"Some say Ayurveda is dependent on *Atharvaveda*. The analogy of four fingers being the *Vedas* and thumb being Ayurveda answers this question of dependency.

"The basis of Ayurveda is *vata, pitta* and *kapha*: these in turn are dependent on two Gods each; *Vata* on Maruth and Akasha, *Pitta* on Agni and Aditya, *Kapha* on Soma and Varuna. Another opinion is that *Satva, Rajas* and *Tamas* are the basis. The physician has to treat the pains or diseases of the past, present and future.

"Any questions?" Kashyapa asked before ending the lesson.

Jivaka asked, "How is Kumarabhrtya different from the other branches?"

"Medicine for children should be palatable, it is not so for adults. Children should not be treated with excessive cleansing measures. They should be treated with only oral medication, ointments and irrigation with drugs. Cold or sweet drugs that do not produce burning sensation should be used. I will describe its intricacies as I proceed with my next lesson!

"Now a question: what are the four pillars of Ayurveda? Can any of you give an answer?" Kashyapa asked.

Chaitanya, the eldest, all of fourteen, answered, "The drugs."

"The next pillar?"

Shiva said, "The patient."

"The next one?"

Deva said, "The physician."

"Next and the last one?"

Jivaka said, "The attendant of the child. If the attendant does not obey the physician's instructions, nothing will come out of the treatment."

"Excellent," said Kashyapa. "And the four pillars of the treatment are..."

The disciples said in unison, "The physician, the drug, the patient and the attendant!"

Samskaras

Kashyapa began, "You may wonder about the rituals that we practise. For example, that of Upanayana that you have witnessed or had been through, so that you become eligible to recite the Gayathri mantra and are bound to recite it every day. Savithri or Gayathri mantra offers salutations to the Sun God. There are some other rituals too, conducted in childhood. These also are rites of passage which every child has to go through.

"These are Jatakarma, Namakarana, Karna Vedhana, Surya and Chandra Parikramana, Chudakarma, Phala and Annaprashana and Upanayana."

Jivaka asked, "Why do we have to have them? These are not treatments!"

Kashyapa elaborated: "A person is born with certain *doshas* and *gunas* inherited from seven generations of his forebears. But what happens after birth is not known or predetermined. The notion that he should develop normally is a major consideration. Hence, the wise people decided on certain rituals at the right time and stages of man's life. This is to ensure that the environment provides opportunity for enhancing the potential given at birth."

Chaitanya: "Do only children have them?"

Kashyapa described at length: "There are sixteen samskaras in a person's life from birth to death. But we will talk about what concerns us—only those in childhood. The first one is soon after birth and it is called Jatakarma.

"After cleaning the body, performing of protective measures, auspicious oblations, keeping the face to the east, the physician should rub gold with a little water, mix with honey and ghee and give it to the infant for licking. Feeding of gold increases intellect, improves digestion and metabolism, improves complexion and eliminates the effects of grahas. The child becomes virtuous as it is auspicious to be fed on gold. Use of gold for one month improves his intelligence and protects from diseases. Use gold for six months—the child can retain whatever he hears.

"Parikramana: Taking the baby outdoors for the first time is done in the fourth month. He is given bath, dressed in new clothes, is taken to the temple. After worshipping fire with ghee and rice, after praying to the Brahmin, Vishnu, Skanda and family Gods with flowers and fragrances, he is taken home.

Here the physician offers a prayer saying, 'Oh child! May you be protected by the blessings of Brahmins, sages and Gods and live for 100 years.'

"In the sixth month, on an auspicious day after worshipping Gods and giving offerings to Brahmins, the physician makes a sacred altar in a clean place in the centre of the house or garden. He keeps bright and colourful ornaments and gems, milk, honey, and various animals made of dough with honey, ghee and toys of clay and recites a hymn of protection.

"Then, after he is bathed and adorned, the child should be made to sit for a short time in the altar and whatever he picks up, he becomes a claimant for it.

"However, the child should not be allowed to sit too long and the objects and the place around him should be safe.

"Phalaprashana: The physician should prescribe feeding of juice of fruit in the sixth month.

"Annaprashana: After the eruption of teeth or in the tenth month, feeding of cereals may be done. This is done on an auspicious day, with the child being made to sit on a sacred altar with delicious foods. The physician sits facing east and the adorned child facing the west. Then, after lighting the fire, the physician offers prayers to Prajapathi. Then he feeds the child three-four mashed balls of food.

"Then the mother is advised gradually to increase the

amounts in small quantities after the twelfth month, and gradually introduce suitable new preparations. I will tell you about the suitable food for the child in detail…

"Piercing of ears of the child requires the physician to be very careful. Knowledge about complications arising due to improper piercing is essential. He has to be an expert and experienced physician. He needs to know the exact place where no bleeding or infections occur.

"Chudakarma or tonsure allows you to examine the head."

Kashyapa continues, "Now you know what you need to know how to set up these rituals, what mantras to recite—as these too fall under the duties of a paediatric physician. I expect you to practise all the necessary hymns and prayers."

Jivaka asked, "These are instructions to the mother or family to do what is appropriate to the age of the child—why do you need mantras and hymns? Can they not be simply instructed?"

Kashyapa asked, "Why do you think we go to so much trouble?"

In unison his students said, "We do not know!"

Kashyapa said, "Let us take your own example. Before the initiation of our lessons, I instructed you to sit in an auspicious place, utter 'Om' and recite Savithri mantra three times. Suppose I had said, 'Come children sit anywhere, anyway you like and listen to what I say'—which one would you prefer?"

All of them said, "Of course, the first one."

Kashyapa asked, "Why? Why not the second method?"

Jivaka said, "Sitting in the right place, after having had bath, puts you in the right frame of mind to start the lessons."

"Why Om?" asked Kashyapa.

Chaitanya said, "Om is sacred. It encompasses the universe and creates resonance between you and the universe. You are ready to receive what the universe gives. It opens your mind and dissolves the difference between you and the world."

Jivaka asked sceptically, "Won't any other sound do as well?

Kashyapa said smilingly, "Like what?"

The other disciples were shocked at Jivaka's arrogance, but the Master seemed merely amused.

Jivaka said softly, realising that he had overstepped "Sa?" the beginning of *ragas*, yet not yielding his point.

Kashyapa said, "Let us experiment with the two sounds. Om and Sa. Now all of you start. Take a deep breath and say Sa." The boys said Sa in unison.

"Again!"

They said it in unison once again.

"Again!"

They said it in unison once again.

"Now let us say Om!"

They started the Om...started at a lower level reaching the crescendo and coming back again.

"Again!"

Again, they said Om in unison.

"Again!"

Again, they said Om in unison.

Kashyapa said, "Jivaka, first you tell me if Sa and Om are the same."

Jivaka said, "Om is definitely better."

Kashyapa said, "It, too, is only a sound."

Jivaka said, "When you say Om, you feel beautiful inside."

Chaitanya said, "You find you are in the world of music —the music that envelops you."

Shiva said, "It felt like waves of the ocean. Low waves rumbling and high waves roaring—and you in the midst enjoying it."

Deva said, "It was like being on the top of a mountain and saying Om once and hearing it echo a hundred times, ending with the softest echo."

Ramdev said, "It felt that I was in the presence of God and praying to him."

Rudra said, "I saw hundreds of colours, like the sunrise, like the rainbow, swirling and enveloping me."

Vatsya, three years older than Jivaka, said, "I felt first a gentle soothing breeze, getting stronger till I was cold and shivering. And then again warm gentle breeze wrapping me up in a cocoon of warmth."

The boys were amazed. They looked at each other. They all had experienced the Om differently.

Kashyapa smiled: "Now you have experienced it. That is important. These may be very different, but each one of you was moved by it. I would call it warming up and getting you ready for your lessons."

"Now, the Gayathri mantra and what it means—you will understand as you grow up. You will give your meaning to it too. But basically you worship the Sun. Even if you don't believe in one or the other god, the Sun is visible, exists and source of light, life and energy. It is easy to pray to him. Jivaka, can you pray to the Sun with full faith?"

Jivaka softly said, "Yes, I can and I will. Everyday with complete faith."

Kashyapa said, "Yes, we will come back to the rituals of samskaras. Rituals have two components: propitiation of evil and facilitation of good forces. For example, at Jatakarma you appease Jataharini, the demoness who harms the mother and the newborn. You pray to the sages, Brahmins and Gods requesting them to bless them. These mantras drive away the fears in the mother and put her in a happy mood. Happiness of the mother is most important to the welfare of the child. For example, keeping the place clean, with fragrance of incense and flowers, sacred chants makes the mother feel secure. As soon as the baby is born the father takes two little pebbles and makes noises in the baby's ears saying, "May you live long. May you be strong like stone..." We know that the baby does not understand it, but its auditory channels are stimulated for the first time. The father feels good about his wishes for his son. So the idea is to put everyone in a happy frame of mind dispelling all the fears."

"Now the next lesson. I want all of you to examine the rituals of samskaras and tell what do these mean? Rituals without understanding the meaning are of no use to the performer and the receiver. Enhanced happy state of mind comes only when the meaning is understood by the performer and receiver."

Story Of Garlic

Kashyapa said, "I will introduce you to the sacred precepts of the classic, as you all are going to study it. In this classic, there are eight sections and 120 chapters. The eight sections are sutra (fundamentals), nidana (diagnosis) vimana (specific features), atmaniscaya (study of human body), indriya (signs of life and death), chikitsa (therapeutics), siddhi (successful management) and kalpa (pharmaceutical preparations).

"Understanding and learning of this is like learning the Vedas and the learning of it is equally virtuous, prolongs life and protects from evil. It provides pleasure, money, respect and fame and leads to emancipation. This is to show the importance of the classic that you are all going to learn.

"But I will not be teaching you the way I would teach a grown-up as you will find it tedious. So let us see how we can study this classic not by simply learning the shlokas by heart, which you must so that it is in you for all time to come, but by trying to understand by linking the present to the past and future. Kala or time is the main God we need to recognise as the most important one for us—the healers of children.

"Today I will start with the story of the lowly garlic that you are familiar with."

Chaitanya said, "Brahmins are barred from eating it!"

Kashyapa said smilingly, "But not from using it as a medicine!"

Jivaka asked, "Why is garlic so important?"

Kashyapa said, "I will tell you the story of Lasuna (garlic) that is only a hearsay story from generations. Lord Indra's wife Shachi did not have a child even for a hundred years. So Indra gave this nectar (garlic juice) to her to drink. Shy and trembling, she drank and it accidentally fell on an unholy place. Indra told Shachi that she will bear many children and that nectar will become a rejuvenating substance for earthly beings. But because of its association with an unholy place, it will have bad smell and will not be used by the Brahmins. Its juice in the pod is pungent, its stem salty and bitter, leaves astringent, in *Vipaka* it is sweet. Sweet, bitter, pungent are predominant in succeeding order. It cures common diseases and increases longevity. It is an appetiser, aphrodisiac and creates a disease-free state. It enhances memory, intellect, strength, complexion and eyesight. It stimulates reproductive systems in men and women."

Jivaka asked, "It can really do all these? But some of the things I did not understand."

Kashyapa said, "At times what you do not understand when you are young, begins to make sense when you are older. All of us see more and different meaning in the same objects as we grow up. Be patient, when you are ready, the knowledge will seek you!"

Chaitanya asked, "Are there medicinal uses of garlic?"

Kashyapa said, "The list is endless but I will tell you a few to start with. You will find that I use it for almost all the disorders. Those with excessive *vata*, skin disorders, eye disorders, indigestion, urinary problems, diseases of bones, in dislocation, fracture and so on.

"However, it should not be used for excessive *kapha* and *pitta*, those with malnutrition, pregnant and nursing woman, after vomiting and diarrhoea, jaundice and those who have received cleansing treatments such as emeses, purgation and so on."

Vatsya said, "It is to be always eaten?"

Kashyapa said, "It is used as food, drink, decoctions, in medicines, as oil and so on."

Kashyapa laughingly said, "If this is not enough, I will tell you about an ancient practice that you will find hilarious. This is called Big Fragrance recommended for the wealthy for driving all diseases away and welcoming good health. The rich person should eat garlic as recommended. He must also wear crown and garlands of garlic, tie bunches over the hands and the feet and keep the same in his clothes and on the bed. He should tie strings of garlic on the doors. All the people in the household too should dress, drink and eat the same way as the master of the house!" Kashyapa paused to see the reactions of the disciples.

The disciples, for once, were not quiet and obedient and burst into laughter.

Jivaka asked laughingly, "Have you ever prescribed it?"

Kashyapa said, "No, but my teacher did for a king!"

They chorused, "And?"

Kashyapa said, "The answer is for you to find out!"

The lesson ended with that instruction. Younger children like Vatsya and Jivaka went outdoors to play. While the older ones stayed indoors to complete the daily chores of the ashram, cleaning, cooking and helping Kashyapa attend to the patients.

Once, the stream of patients ended and everyone was getting ready for lunch, Chaitanya asked, "May I ask a question?"

Kashyapa sensed a problem brewing, but he said, "Of course."

Chaitanya said, "Is Jivaka not too young to learn all the lessons that you are teaching? I came to you only after I was ten. You have said you will take pupils who are ten years old."

Kashyapa said, "You are right. But I had no option, as he

is a foundling left in my care. How can I prevent him from learning everything simply by observing."

Chaitanya said nothing.

Kashyapa asked Chaitanya, "Has his being here bothered you in any way?"

Chaitanya conceded, "He is a nice kid. But it feels odd to compete with a five-year-old, when you ask questions and he gives the answers."

Kashyapa said mischievously, "Especially when he is right?"

Kashyapa added, "Don't worry about him Chaitanya, you all have families and parents. He and I have no one. I am grooming him to take care of me when I am old. You can see that I am no longer getting younger."

Chaitanya understood the situation better, and felt that he should apologise for his impertinence as the Master was so honest.

Kashyapa stopped him from offering apologies.

"It is a closed chapter. It is natural for everyone to wonder about Jivaka, but I would rather not spend my time explaining his presence to everybody. Perhaps you could do that on my behalf" Chaitanya nodded his head.

Later, as the boys were leaving for their homes, Kashyapa saw them getting into a huddle. He guessed that the problem was solved for the time being.

Jivaka went around the ashram, completely unaware of what was happening.

Kashyapa, at night told Jivaka what had transpired.

Jivaka said, "Why should my age matter? We are here to learn!"

Kashyapa said, "You are right. But people have their own way of looking at events and issues."

Jivaka sighed. "Tata, but will you keep me as your disciple no matter what people say?"

"Of course, Jivaka, as far as you are concerned, you were my disciple when you came to this ashram when you were three. Now, when you are five, you are my disciple. And always and forever you will be—till you decide that you no longer desire to be my disciple. For me, you are my only disciple." Kashyapa and Jivaka exchanged one of their rare hugs.

The Ultimate Test

As Kashyapa was busy with the patients, an emissary from a group of physicians from Varanasi arrived. After attending to his needs following a long journey, Kashyapa asked him about the purpose of his visit. The young man was a disciple of Pramati Bhargava, who was famed for his view that there is only one disease because all illnesses have a common appearance. Indeed, this was contested by most physicians, yet he was well respected as a great clinician. The young disciple, however, was most reluctant to divulge the reason for his visit. After much gentle persuasion, finally Kashyapa was able to find out the reason. Eminent scholars had discovered that Sage Kashyapa was training a child as a paediatrician, a thing unheard of by the physicians. So they had decided to challenge the notion that a child can be trained. They had decided to come to Kashyapa's ashram and examine the child to test the veracity of the claim that the child, indeed, was qualified.

Kashyapa said, "I don't need anybody's approval. The boy is only learning. He is not practising."

The disciple said, "Lord Kashyapa, Sir...They are very disturbed by the very fact that you have formally anointed him as a disciple. According to them, even this is not acceptable. They can and will probably allow it if they can satisfy themselves that he is indeed knowledgeable in the basics of the practice of Ayurveda!"

Kashyapa was firm. "I am not interested in proving it to anyone! It is between me and the boy!"

The disciple said hastily, "Lord Kashyapa, by not allowing the test, they will think you are afraid that the boy will fail the test!"

Kashyapa said, "I don't care! I am not going to expose a young child to these people who could themselves be scholars or charlatans!" He was getting somewhat angry and that indeed was unusual for him!

Jivaka, who was a silent bystander, said, "Master, may I say something?"

Kashyapa said, "Go ahead."

Jivaka said, "Master, it will be an honour for me to be tested by such eminent people. If I pass, it will be a credit to my teacher. If I fail, they will say it is all right, I am only a child and I have a long way to go and it is true! Either way, there is nothing to lose!"

Kashyapa said, "You really want it? I really don't care for it. I am teaching you, not for examination. It is because of your desire to learn."

Jivaka said, "It will be a great honour for me to be tested by such eminent physicians. Please Master, please invite them. It would be a great occasion for us here to meet all those whom we only know by name!"

Finally, Kashyapa wrote a letter to the physicians.

"Respected physicians, it is indeed an honour for us here at this ashram that you have decided to pay us a visit. Though I am not inclined to put young Jivaka through the test that you will set up for him, he is very keen to be examined by such great people like you. With humility I invite you all to my ashram and offer my humble abode on the banks of the sacred Ganga and my simple hospitality to the best of my austere existence."

Months passed from spring to autumn. Somewhere in the middle of winter, the visiting scholars arrived. The Ganga was frozen on the surface and appeared as if she had lost all movement. The trees looked bare and gaunt, having shed all their leaves. Only the vegetable patch behind the ashram tended by Kashyapa and Jivaka was green, with winter vegetables thriving, ready to be harvested.

One fine day, Kashyapa and Jivaka returned from the banks of the Ganga at dawn, Kashyapa after meditation and Jivaka from play. The physicians and their entourage of disciples arrived on horses, with porters and also food supplies as they believed that Kashyapa may not have sufficient provisions for such a large group. Kashyapa, Jivaka and other disciples received them with great humility. Among them were indeed great minds of the time. Vayovrida, Kankayana, Krishna Bharadwaja, Rajarishi, Rishi Sabhaya, Hiranyakhya Vaideha and Pramati Bhargava himself.

Jivaka and the other disciples were amazed at their having come all the way to test Jivaka. Whilc Jivaka was respectful though unfazed, the other disciples were curious to witness the great event of the century. As the entourage reached, people from the nearby ashrams slowly arrived to witness the test. Almost everyone except Richika was there. Richika, as usual, was too immersed in his own work to even notice what was going on in Kashyapa's ashram.

The travellers bathed in the hot water provided by the ashram and partook of the simple meal provided by Kashyapa. They also took the sweetmeats and fruit they had brought in honour of Kashyapa.

Kashyapa was polite and aloof. The physicians mistook him to be fearful of the outcome of the test. Kashyapa asked the disciples to prepare eight elevated seats covered with deer skins. Kashyapa sprinkled the seats with sacred water of the Ganga and prayed for their welfare and long life.

In front of them on the ground on a bed of darbha grass, Jivaka was told to sit. Immediately Jivaka came to Kashyapa, touched his feet. Kashyapa lifted him up and said in his ears: "My blessings are always with you. I know you can do it. But you really don't have to. I have neither faith nor stake in these foolish gambles."

Jivaka whispered, "But I want to... I need to...." Jivaka went to each of the physicians and touched their feet. Grudgingly they blessed Jivaka. "Shall we begin?" Pramati Bhargava asked. Kashyapa nodded.

Pramati Bhargava: "A simple question to start with. How many branches are there in Ayurveda?"

Jivaka said "Eight."

"And these are?"

"Kumarabhrtya (Childcare), Shalaka Tantra (Ear, Nose and Throat), Agadha Tantra (Toxicology), Vajikarana (Eugenics), Kayachikitsa (Internal Medicine) Shalya Tantra (Surgery), Jarachikitsa (Gerontology) and Bhuta Vidya (Psychological Medicine)."

"What else is included in Kumarabhrtya?"

"Prasuti Tantra and Striroga—but I have not learnt these..."

Now Vayovrida started. "How many types of diseases are there?"

Jivaka sat up straight and said, "Honourable Pramati Bhargava says there is only one; your eminence believes that there are two types: exogenous and endogenous; honourable Kankayana says diseases can be divided into three groups based on prognosis: curable, difficult to cure and incurable. Rishi

Krishna Bharadwaja divides them into four types: exogenous and three caused by *vata, pitta* and *kapha*. Rajarishi Daruvaha divides them into five, adding one more to Rishi Krishna Bharadwaja's four, namely combination of *vata, pitta* and *kapha* as yet another type. Rishi Sabhaya says there are six types according to six tastes of eatables and drinkables. Rishi Hiranykshya believes that these are seven in number depending on single *dosha*, two of the three and combination of all the three. Master Vaideha Nimi named eight types by adding exogenous to the above seven."

The physicians nodded their surprised approval. "And what does Sage Kashyapa believe?" they chorused.

Jivaka said "Bhagavan Kashyapa believes that there are only two, endogenous and exogenous, and these are detailed in so many different ways."

"And you, Jivaka—what do you think?" a trick question indeed by the wily physicians.

Jivaka said, "I can only elaborate on what Bhagavan says: diseases are innumerable due to equilibrium, decreased and increased status of the *doshas*!"

Kashyapa's face glowed with pride, while the visiting physicians looked incredulously at each other. Vayovrida continued "Why are diseases innumerable?"

Jivaka said, "Because of the causes, nature, locations and qualities perceived by five senses, psyche and the specific treatments."

Kankayana: "You said 'psyche'? How does that come in?"

Jivaka said, "Honourable Kankayana, the site of diseases are two—psyche that is mind and the body. Both are interacting forces. Mind and body are not separate entities. The *doshas* are very important while the *gunas* namely, Rajasik, Tamasik and Satvik are equally important for healing."

Rajarishi Daruvaha asked, "In children what is considered a predominant mode?"

"*Kapha*, Sir! But it still is a *dosha* leading to disease. The *satva*, on the other hand, of the Trigunas is the most desirable, as it is a protective factor unlike the Tridosha Rajas and Tamas."

Hiranakshya continued the examination. "Is Ayurveda a science?"

"Yes, it is, because it follows the scientific principles laid down by sankhya!"

"And these are...?"

"Prathyaksha (what you see), Anumana (inference), Upamana (similarities) and Shabda (the word)."

"Are there unscientific practices in (the word) Ayurveda?"

"Yes...but!"

Kashyapa thought it best to interrupt at this stage, for the attacking physicians to regroup and give some respite to little Jivaka. Jivaka was midway through the examination of the scientific nature of Ayurveda.

Kashyapa offered some sweetmeats brought by the physicians, with bela fruit juice which they gladly ate. Kashyapa absented himself in the pretext of attending to some medicinal decoction being brewed. The visitors got into a huddle, thinking of trick questions that could trip this genius child. Defeat him they must! You cannot allow a child to be a physician at such a young age. It is a sacrilege. They must test him like they would test an adult. There should be no lowering of the bar. They conspired to set a trap, no matter what the outcome be!

They re-assembled.

"Describe the nature of Tridosha." Jivaka elaborated easily and convincingly.

"Does the foetus have mind and consciousness?"

"Yes" and Jivaka went on to describe the various features over the nine months of pregnancy. Jivaka did it to the satisfaction of the inquisitors.

They asked him about seasons, diets, various treatments and so on.

They also asked him about the various *samskaras*.

"What is the difference between *samskaras* described in Grhyasutras and Kumarabhrtya?"

Jivaka thought over it, as he had not pondered over it earlier and said, "Karnavedhana as a samskara is not part of the Grhyasutras. So...piercing of ears is an important samskara in Kumarabhrtya. I believe it has a medical connotation."

"Really, It is simply ornamental, is it not?"

Jivaka insisted, "No, it has a clear set of instructions: how to let the rays of the sun pass through ear lobes and piercing to be done after sterilising the needle in the spot where there are no veins or nerves. It has to have a medical reason."

They jeered! "What would it be?"

Jivaka was first silent, then looked at Kashyapa and then faced his inquisitors and said, "It is a procedure for immunising the child for the future!"

There was a stunned silence. The inquisitors could go no further with this child prodigy.

One final test: Pramati Bhargava announced his verdict: "If he qualifies in the last test, they will unanimously pronounce him a paediatrician."

Kashyapa said, "And that is?"

Pramati Bhargava declared, "Physical endurance and faith in oneself is an important aspect of a physician."

In this final test, Jivaka should submerge himself in the holy waters of the Ganga, stay down for ten minutes and then come up!

Kashyapa lost his cool. "No—never. He is only a child. I do not care if you don't declare him a physician. I withdraw my hospitality and insist that you all are welcome to leave!"

Offended, the inquisitors stood up to leave!

Aghast, they saw Jivaka running with his tousled head towards the Ganga. Before anybody could say a word or act, he jumped into the frozen Ganga from a boulder ashore!

Kashyapa was distraught. He rushed towards the bank crying out, "No... Jivaka...no...Jivaka." By the time he reached the banks—others too followed him—Jivaka was no longer to be seen. Kashyapa sat on a rock, his face covered with his palms. "Oh my God, how could this have happened?

I should have anticipated this cruelty in these heartless men—subjecting the child to this hard test, and I curse myself for failing to protect my divine child." The was totally distraught.

Everyone was shocked at the cruelty of the famous physicians. It was obvious that they had come with the intent of finishing off Jivaka psychologically and physically.

Ten minutes later, there was a sudden hush. A small grey head emerged out of the thin layer of shimmering ice. Up came a very wet Jivaka, blithely swimming towards the sand banks. The boy emerged from the Ganga, with the icicles hanging from his ringlets of hair, giving him the appearance of grey matted locks. His face and limbs were wrinkled due to prolonged immersion in water. He did appear like a wizened old man. The sages, astounded, shouted in unison, "The wise old man! Vriddha Jivaka!"

That moment, when Kashyapa saw Jivaka emerge safely and alive out of the Ganga, was etched forever in the sage's mind. Kashyapa rushed to him joyously, "Oh my child! What have you done? You almost killed me with this game of yours." Kashyapa wrapped Jivaka in his blanket and ran to the ashram. Jivaka's teeth were chattering as he whispered, "I am used to holding my breath under water, even in winter. I have been playing this game for a long time, behind your back! I know you would not have let me!"

"Oh, you silly boy! come now, have a hot bath and some hot milk. I nearly died of fright!" Kashyapa added.

Jivaka was indeed contrite. "I am sorry, but I hated the way they wanted to humiliate you! I cannot let you down—after all I am your favourite disciple," he smiled cheekily.

Later on, when Kashyapa brought Jivaka after a hot bath, all wrapped in coarse white cloth, they could see that he still was the same young Jivaka. They all had concurred that he, indeed, was wise beyond his years. He deserved to be called wise and therefore, old. They decided to confer the title "Vriddha Jivaka" in recognition of his wisdom and knowledge.

The inquisitors had the grace to accept defeat. They sat Jivaka on a pedestal where Pramati Bhargava originally sat, wrapped his own woven gold shawl of famous Varanasi silk around Jivaka, garlanded him and declared, "We unanimously pronounce you to be Vriddha Jivaka, a physician with no parallel. May you bring glory to your teacher Sage Kashyapa."

Then they departed for Varanasi.

After everyone left, Kashyapa and Jivaka sat next to the fire laughing at the turn of events. Kashyapa then said, "Jivaka, what you have acquired so far is knowledge. It is time from here onwards to acquire wisdom. Knowledge is easy to acquire if you are bright. But wisdom comes only with effort and pain."

"Yes, Master." Jivaka stooped down to touch Kashyapa's feet in reverence. Jivaka knew that he could fool anyone with knowledge, but wisdom was what Kashyapa would help him to attain!

Further Lessons

The morning after Jivaka was renamed Vriddha Jivaka, Kashyapa took him to Richika's ashram. Richika was delighted with Kashyapa's rare visits. He could barely see the outlines of Kashyapa and Jivaka as his vision was deteriorating fast. The old man had been terribly excited about something happening in Kashyapa's ashram. But Richika was immersed in his studies. He thought, "It must be something important if it has brought the sage himself to my ashram."

Kashyapa very briefly described what had happened the previous day. Richika roared with laughter—first time ever, thought Kashyapa.

"Good for you, my boy Jivaka! Now you can compete with us old people and win too!"

Kashyapa said, "I have a request. The boy is hungry for knowledge. My knowledge is limited to paediatrics. Could you instruct him on the Upanishads in which you indeed excel?"

"Really? Jivaka, do you think you can cope?" Richika said.

Jivaka: "To the best of my ability, Master. In the evening hours, I don't have much to do, so I play."

Ramananda was at the door, watching the drama unfolding. He knew that Jivaka was Richika's son. But he did not know if Kashyapa knew it or not. If he knew it, he must have withheld the information for a good reason. Ramananda himself did not tell Richika because he was like a child himself, especially with his failing vision. How could he take care of a child? Over the last two years, he had seen the strong bond developing between Sage Richika and the boy. What happened the previous day went far beyond his mother's dream. Ramananda had wondered about her, when the child turned up at Kashyapa's ashram, a three-year-old turning up exactly three years and nine months after he threw the girl out of Richika's ashram.

Richika said, "My vision is bothering me. It may be good for me to have the little one around. I never thought you would have such a disciple when I saw this little mite two years back. I never thought I would have such a distinguished disciple. Indeed, it would be good to challenge my ageing brain."

Settling Jivaka with Richika, Kashyapa came back to his

ashram. He called all his other disciples who were loitering around pretending to be busy. They came and sat at his feet.

"Now that the whole drama is over—with no loss to me or Jivaka—I want to know who was behind all this? I have almost waited for six months to find out the root of this, ever since the emissary came from Varanasi. I just wanted to see how it played out…Now Chaitanya, you are the oldest. Tell me how what transpires in this little ashram would reach the great medicine men in Varanasi?"

Chaitanya was silent.

Kashyapa said, "If you tell the truth, no matter how bad your action may be, I will continue to teach you. But if I don't get to the bottom of the matter, none of you are going to be my disciple from today onwards."

Chaitanya said, "Master, when I started this, I did not dream of these repercussions. Let me begin from the beginning: when our lesson started, you did warn us about our resentment towards Jivaka because he was so good. But the ambers of jealousy continued to smoulder. We discussed endlessly, all of us except Vatsya, how to humiliate Jivaka. Sir, please believe me when I say that we in our ignorance thought it was only Jivaka's humiliation that we wanted. We did not even dream, how it could reflect on you.

"When my father, himself a scholar, was going away to Varanasi, I had told him how you were taking a little child as a disciple and how Jivaka was showing off all the time. My father believes that I have a great potential as a physician of children. So when in Varanasi, he kept telling people how his own son was being neglected by Lord Kashyapa and how he was hoodwinked by his foster son. This grew to be an ugly rumour in scholarly circles. They simply could not believe that a person of the Master's reputation was tainted by such unscholarly act.

"When they sent the emissary, my father thought that the Master would apologise and say that Jivaka was his foster son and nothing more." Kashyapa sighed, "That is when things moved beyond your planning…"

"Master, please forgive us. We now know that Jivaka deserves all those accolades!"

Kashyapa said, "You are young, but Chaitanya, your father should have known better. Never mind. Remember, jealousy is a destructive emotion. The first thing it does is to destroy your learning by putting blinkers on you. Think of him as Vriddha Jivaka, an old man. Not a child, as you have seen him emerging out of the Ganga, wrinkled and grey-haired. That image will allow you to cope with your jealousies."

The disciples, contrite, repeatedly begged for forgiveness and went to their homes.

Jivaka came back with sparkling eyes. "Sage Richika told me the story of Nachiketa—it was such a beautiful story. He was like me—was he not? Do you think my mother, I mean my birth mother, was like Nachiketa's mother?"

Kashyapa said gently, "I am sure she was…"

Next morning when the disciples came, Kashyapa and Jivaka were playing chess. Chaitanya came, touched Kashyapa's feet as usual and then came to touch Jivaka's feet. Shocked, Jivaka jumped up, "Oh my God! What are you doing Chaitanya—what is this new and strange behaviour?" He ran away from them laughing. "You know, I am your friend and playmate. Yesterday's thing was all drama. It was a stunt I pulled because I could not bear them insulting our Master! Our life continues in the ashram as before. Ask the Master if you like!"

Kashyapa smilingly accepted Jivaka's statement. He thought to himself: Honour sits lightly on this little head!

The lessons continued as before.

Kashyapa picked up from where he had stopped the discussions deliberately. "Jivaka, you said yesterday that there were many unscientific practices in Ayurveda?"

Jivaka: "I was wrong, Master, there are unscientific theories but not really practices as such. But unscientific theories may lead to unscientific practices!"

"What would you call unscientific?"

Jivaka said, "Please forgive me. But these may go against what you have taught or what you may teach in future."

Kashyapa said, "I want you to be honest and free. You have equal chance of being right while you give some examples...."

Jivaka said, "For example, you set score on predicting what the person is going to be, based on physical features. I am not convinced of it. You attribute *balarogas* to *balagrahas*. Then these grahas are personified as some kind of demonesses or demons. In the absence of knowledge of aetiology, we are attributing the diseases to demonic forces. Suppose you don't believe in the supernatural, like me? How do you explain the aetiology?"

Kashyapa said, "If you don't believe, they don't exist—right? But if the patient believes and healer believes, it is all right. In your case, if the patient believes but you don't believe, what would you do?"

Jivaka: "Yes, Master. Faith of the patient is an important component. Even if I don't believe, I need to respect the patient's belief. Master—tell me why you tell us many myths, extraordinary stories—to show us the world of beliefs that surrounds us. I had always wondered why you told these stories! Thank you, Master. I have always enjoyed those stories—but never thought there were reasons for which you told us the stories."

Jivaka continued, "Master, you have told us many examples of dream interpretations, they look too farfetched to me. For example, a nursing mother having bad dreams, warns of illness in the infant..."

Kashyapa said, "I do believe that the dreams dredge the deepest of our joys and fears and also can reach out to the future, linking with the past in ways unknown to the conscious mind. Dreams are the best example of the mind going beyond time and space."

Jivaka pondered, "Is there any way of proving it?"

Kashyapa said, "You can keep a dream diary and over a period, examine it for its predictive or healing power!"

"Healing power?"

"Yes, I believe it has a healing power too."

"Yes, we will keep our dream diaries and see what comes out of it!"

The disciples dispersed to attend to their chores.

Kashyapa was wondering about Jivaka's energy and interest. Perhaps he needs more things to keep him engaged. "Jivaka, we are in the best place in the whole world for someone who wants to learn. Are there things you want to learn that Richika and I cannot help you with?"

Jivaka's eyes widened with pleasure "Really? Can I learn something I like to? I love music. I remember hearing it somewhere—maybe in my dreams!"

Kashyapa said "What? Where would you have heard music?"

"I don't know. I was blissful hearing the singing and the strumming of the tanpura!"

"I am sure I will find a good teacher for you. But it will take away what little time you have left to play."

"But this is different. I want to learn."

Thus began his *sadhana* for music under a master who initially was reluctant to teach such a young boy. The fact that he was given the title Vriddha Jivaka bothered everybody, including the prospective teacher. Once he started the lessons, there was no stopping the sadhana. To get a better idea of *talas* (rhythms) he insisted in learning the tabla. Everyone was amazed by the boundless energy and commitment the child had for everything he did.

Reunion

Now all of fifteen, Jivaka was grinding the medicinal preparation that he had picked from the forests and dried under the blazing summer sun. It was hot and sultry, with a promise of thunderstorms and the Ganga rearing to go on the rampage.

Kashyapa was reading some palm leaves, trying to answer the question whether a particular treatment, especially giving of enema, was suitable for children or not. It was indeed a controversial issue yet to be settled. Jivaka had made up his mind that he was against it. Intuitively. But was yet to marshal his arguments in a lucid manner.

Jivaka felt a presence at a distance under the tamarind tree. It was a young man—hesitant, looking at Jivaka, yet not approaching him. Jivaka laid down the pestle and walked towards the tamarind tree. Jivaka was now a strapping youngster with curly, shoulder-length hair, his fair skin turned copper because of the long hours he had spent outdoors, finding roots and herbs, tending the vegetable garden and, of course, swimming in the Ganga hours together, challenging the strong waves and whirlpools through summers and winters.

Jivaka broke into a run, a broad smile lighting up his face. He shouted "Yadu, my brother, how nice to see you, come, come with me. Why are you standing here?"

Yadu, his playmate of childhood, shyly shrugged while Jivaka enveloped him in a bear hug. Yadu murmured, "I did not know if I can approach you, now that you are a famous physician!"

Jivaka said, "Oh that! Come, come. What news of my mother? Father? Rest of you, my brothers and sisters? It is wonderful that you have come. I hope everybody is okay at home! I went looking for our old home. You must have moved away a long time ago. The little temple was still there. All dilapidated but the Tata was no longer there."

Yadu said simply, "Mother is dying. She wanted to see you—we tried to dissuade her, saying that you won't want to meet us!"

Jivaka: "How can you think like that about me? Of course, I will come with you to see my mother! Let me tell my Master and then we will be off!"

Kashyapa had seen the whole drama under the tamarind tree and had guessed that the stranger probably was the washerwoman's son. He had always sensed how Jivaka had missed his foster parents and siblings, though he hardly spoke about them. How disappointed he was three years ago when he went looking for them relying on his memory. Jivaka took Yadu by hand, they both bowed and touched Kashyapa's feet. Jivaka said, "Master, Mother is dying. She wants to see me. I want to meet her and thank her. May I go?"

Kashyapa: "Of course. She is a good woman. Please thank her for the gift she has given me."

Yadu and Jivaka both looked up in surprise. 'Gift?' Kashyapa said, "Yes, you Jivaka. What else can I call you?" Jivaka was deeply touched. Impulsively he went and hugged Kashyapa, one of those rare events indeed. Neither of them were demonstrative by nature.

It is about to rain. The parched dusty earth, dry, thirsty, quivering leaves await it. No sign of relief, air still devoid of even the slightest stirring of breeze. Breathless, you gape at the blue skies, the meandering Ganga blue with grey. The air is still, the parched earth silent. Suddenly the breeze starts like a huge tide. It keeps coming in tides on parched earth, battering the sheesham trees which sway helplessly.

The clouds gather, lightning strikes beyond the mountains in silence. The rain lashes down on the parched earth. Fearful yet happy, the trees sway violently, endlessly, hours on end, tirelessly. Then suddenly it stops. Cool and blissful.

There is a glow behind the mountain, and the ethereal Ganga flows silently, gathering up sins.

The storm had just passed beyond the mountains, so the boys decided it would be safer to walk than hire a boat. They were both healthy and young. They walked one whole day and the night, and then they were home.

Neela was no longer a sturdy, healthy woman. She looked frail. Her face lit up with joy at the sight of Jivaka. "Oh my baby! Oh my baby! how handsome you have grown to be. Now I can die in peace. I knew you are already a famous physician—at such a young age. Your mother, your birth mother, dreamt this as you were being born. Her life continues in you, Jivaka."

...then she fell silent—like a lamp burning bright before getting exhausted. Jivaka knew. He went to the Ganga, brought some water in his cupped palms and poured it into Neela's mouth. He signalled to the rest to do the same. Neela went away in peace.

Jivaka had not had time to tell Neela about her gift to Kashyapa. But like all mothers, he was sure she knew that already. Jivaka was at peace that he could participate in the family rituals and the cremation. He could sense the diffidence of the family, with this Brahmin physician participating in the rituals of the low-caste family. Except for the fact that he looked very different—they felt he was, as always, the boy of that household. The four sisters were now all married, well settled. They said shyly, "Thanks to you, the gold helped."

He laughed and slapped them on their backs. "Gold is for

girls, not for boys!" He sat with them and they all had a simple meal. Yadu recalled, "When you came home with my mother, she said that we were not to cook meat at home because you were a Brahmin. We hated it. But once you became our brother, it did not matter, because we all loved you. My mother told us you were someone special, meant for great things unlike us. First it had hurt, but once we got to know you, we found you were like us and we loved you like one amongst us. You never behaved as if you were a special person."

Jivaka said, "Of course I am not. I am like you. I would have been happy staying with all of you all my life. But some promise that our mother pledged, took me to Sage Kashyapa. I am not complaining. But life in the ashram is lonely. With you, it was all fun. How we used to play the whole time, remember!"

Yadu started reminiscing about the things they did, the mischief they got into... "You were quite a naughty three–year-old." Time flew as they recalled and laughed—for Jivaka was once again part of the family.

Then he sighed and stood up. "I better get back! The sage is getting on in years. He needs help in preparing medicine and sometimes, in seeing patients. There is another sage in the ashram next to ours. Sage Richika. He is almost blind. I spend a lot of time, learning from him and reading out to him. He has a helper who is even older than him. They both are equally frail."

Yadu: "That seems rather dreary, living with all those old people! What do you do for fun?" They all laughed.

Jivaka said with a straight face, "I read!"

"Stay with us longer. We wish the circumstance was different that brought you here. Our mother always brooded about you, whether you were happy at the ashram. She said that her promise she made to a dying mother was the most important thing. She also said that you were strong-minded enough to leave the ashram if you did not like it. But she did not want the choice made easy by being in a place where we could be traced and you would come easily to us. She was so proud of you when she heard the stories about your being a famous physician! She would say, "See, I am right. That boy is destined for great things like his mother said he was."

Jivaka asked longingly, "Did she say anything about my mother? My father?"

Neela's husband, now old and stooped said, "She would never talk about the whole episode. Perhaps your mother did not say much to her either as she lay dying. But I was angry inside when she chose to help your mother instead of being with her own family, her own flesh and blood! But now I feel that she had greater vision of things than us, the poor country folk."

Jivaka said, "She used to call me the divine child. I always felt that she was the divine mother!" He stood up.

"I must really go—now the storm has let up. I will hire a boat and go. Please visit me if you can. I have a feeling that I am needed there more than ever now!"

Passage To Tapovan

When Jivaka returned, he fell into brooding silence. Kashyapa noticed it, yet said nothing. Kashyapa was simply watching him, wondering how much to tell the boy. Perhaps as little as possible till it became inevitable. Why burden the young one when already, he appeared to be carrying the whole world on his young shoulders.

Jivaka surfaced from his gloom and came to Kashyapa and said, "My brothers say I was very naughty and they were very happy with me. My mother was proud of what she thinks I have achieved. She died happy, seeing that the promise she made to my dying birth mother was kept."

Kashyapa said, "I am glad, my child." So rarely did Kashyapa call him that, Jivaka felt the vacuum in his heart, created at leaving his family, fill up.

Life was back to normal. Early morning hours with Sage Richika reading, discussing and writing laboriously on palm leaves with the stylus what was dictated. Richika was forever preparing his commentary on the Upanishads.

Later in the day, he worked with Kashyapa in his preparation of medicines, seeing patients along with him. It was continuous work. Recently, Jivaka had decided that Kashyapa's work should be compiled in his lifetime. There were many Kashyapas: the toxicologists, the physicians for adults, references in Buddhist texts to a Kassapa. The life work of his Master should be preserved for posterity. But where was the time? He should sleep less and start working on it.

"Master, will you permit me to compile your work and write it all down? After all, there is only one paediatrician amongst all the Ayurvedic physicians that I know of."

Kashyapa laughed and said, "Oh, people will say...that Sage Kashyapa of yore, handed it down to humans. Only with divine help, it will be considered masterly and generally acceptable."

Jivaka said, "No... No...I don't want it to be of divine origin. I don't know if God exists or not!"

Kashyapa was aghast! "What? You don't believe in God?"

Jivaka said, "I don't have any proof that God exists. But I do believe that he exists in the hearts of people with faith.

That is what matters. Whether I believe or not is immaterial."

Kashyapa fell silent. "Have you discussed this with Richika?"

"No! Should I? Is he an authority on God? I know he is a great scholar of *Vedas* and *Upanishads*. I have learnt much from him. Probably I will ask him when the time is right. He seems to be in a state of tremendous pressure to finish his present commentary. I wonder why. When he dictates, he goes so fast, that sometimes I cannot keep up with him. Fortunately he cannot see me struggling! He is almost completely blind now."

Kashyapa sighed, "Poor man! his health too is failing. As you grow older the sense of urgency takes over—you know that you have little time left to complete what you want to… Sometimes I, too, feel like that!"

Jivaka was stunned. It is true: the folly of youth to believe that you have all the time in the world!

Jivaka suddenly asked Kashyapa, "Is there something you always wanted to do but did not or for some reason could not!"

Kashyapa: "Yes! But now it is too late. I left it too late!"

Jivaka said, "What is it you want to do, Tata?" He lapsed to calling him by the name he addressed him, when he came to him as a toddler. In his mind he was always his Tata.

Kashyapa said dreamily, "I always wanted to go to the four 'dhamas', Gangotri, Yamunotri, Badri and Kedar. From Gangotri to Tapovan and before Badri, to a sacred glacier valley where all the flowers in the world and medicinal plants grow. I should have gone when I was your age. But my Guru was so strict that it was work all the time. Now as my body fails, my mind wants to fly!"

Jivaka said, "I will take you. I can take you."

Kashyapa said, "I cannot walk so much and climbing the Himalayas may be beyond me!"

"I will take you. We will take the mules on the plains. Once in the mountains I will carry you. I too want to see all that when I can. You have me. How do I know if I will have someone at my old age? We shall go!"

Kashyapa's facc lit up "Not a bad idea. As a reward you can be a scribe for compilation of my work," he joked, something he rarely did. Jivaka said "Master, thank you—but please let me write it my way—as you teach and as I learn. Not like the other Samhitas: boring and terse."

Kashyapa laughed. "Don't let others hear you say that. You are an audacious child! Scholarly works are supposed to be dry and boring. Otherwise you will be considered a frivolous scholar. I leave the choice to you. You are the scribe, you decide how you want to write."

"I will write only after the day's work is over. I won't let it come in the way of our work, nor master Richika's work."

Kashyapa light-heartedly said, "When shall we leave for pilgrimage? Oh! Can I call it a pilgrimage when you don't believe in God?"

Jivaka said seriously, "God resides in the waters of the Ganga, the mountains of the mighty Himalayas, in anything good, beautiful and moral."

Kashyapa fell silent at the words of this fifteen-year-old.

Jivaka added "It is the height of summer now. Right time to go on a pilgrimage. The sands of Muni ke Reti is inhabited by lay pilgrims and itinerant sanyasis. Let us go. We don't need much. Some blankets and we stop and eat what we get. Is it alright for you?"

Kashyapa said "For a view of the mighty Himalayas and the valleys, I shall be willing to starve." Jivaka suddenly saw the genius youth behind the ancient face of Kashyapa.

Next morning came a calamity. The old caretaker of Richika did not wake up in the morning. When Richika went to wake him up, he was stone cold. Richika said, "Poor man, his time has come. He passed away peacefully," bowed his head and sat on the ground, holding his hands, relishing the love the old man had showered on him.

Jivaka came at his usual time, hoping to break the news of the pilgrimage. He found Richika holding the hands of his caretaker.

Jivaka took in the scene and gently escorted Richika to Kashyapa. Then he set about doing what was needed, calling the people from other ashrams. First, however, he sent words to the old man's family. With the help of other ashramites, Jivaka bathed Ramananda's body in the Ganga, wrapped it in a new cloth. Only then he called Kashyapa and Richika to pay the last respects.

Richika was most grateful, yet everyone knew that life was going to be hard on the near-blind scholar. Ramananda's relatives arrived in haste, as Jivaka had summoned them. His son lit the pyre. After the cremation on the banks of the Ganga, the son of the old man came, touched Richika's feet and said "My father had sent word only last week that I must bring someone to help you around." Richika had no words. "I have only my son, no other children. But I will leave him with you till you find a disciple or someone to help you."

"You have other children?"

"No Sir. I wish I had but no, we have only this boy. He is about twelve years old."

Richika had not realised how dependent he was on the old man who was no more. He, however, was not worried about himself. His mission in life of completing the commentaries was over, thanks to Kashyapa's boy. He sighed.

Since the grandson of Ramananda had taken over the duties of the old man, Kashyapa and Jivaka were not so worried now about Richika, not that he was their responsibility.

Next morning, as Jivaka completed scribing Richika commentary, he said, "Master, I am glad, this task is over. I need a break. I plan to take my teacher for a pilgrimage of the four dhamas!"

"What? Oh yes, Gangotri, Yamunotri, Badri, Kedar. To me it sounds like a divine chant. I wish I could go—now it is too late. I cannot walk. Worse than that, I cannot see." Jivaka was astounded. What deep yearnings, unfulfilled dreams reside in one's heart. If unexpressed these lie buried, never to be fulfilled. Why don't people say it aloud, before it is too late?

Why should one's dream be buried? Why should one not think and talk about it? Who knows, it may come true. The world has an innate sense of completeness. Man belongs to this world. The world to contribute to man's wholeness.

Jivaka said, "You too could come with us. I can take you too."

Richika laughed. "You silly boy. I know you mean well. How can you take two old people, that too one blind, to the most strenuous and difficult journeys in the mighty Himalayas?"

Jivaka said softly, "Shravana did!" alluding to the story of the devout son who carried his old parents on a pilgrimage.

Richika was speechless. He wished he could see this boy. He sounded so grown-up and mature. He only remembered the little toddler whom Kashyapa had taken to his home. At that time, he had thought Kashyapa was a fool. Now he had been proven wrong. At fifteen, Jivaka was as great a scholar as both him and Kashyapa put together. Perhaps Kashyapa did have the Jnana chakshu (the divine eye of knowledge), he is rumoured to have. Already Richika was in Jivaka's debt for being such a fine scribe and for reading out to him.

Now this? Offer of taking him on a pilgrimage. He was deeply moved by the boy's unconditional devotion. He said, "Come here close to me, Jivaka. I want to see you. I want to feel your face!" Jivaka felt embarrassed but knew that Richika just wanted to see him. He went closer. Richika said, "I have never touched anyone's face before except once, that was a long time ago—please don't mind. I want to see in my mind how you look!" He stroked Jivaka's hair, with both hands felt his face, eyes, nose and mouth gently and held his shoulders and ended up at Jivaka's folded hands.

"Thank you!" He sighed, "I cannot see anything. Even if you carry me, what is the use?"

Jivaka said, "I will be your eyes! I will describe to you all that we see. I promise!"

Richika mumbled, "He will be your eyes!"

"What?" asked Jivaka.

"Nothing! Something someone said long time ago—the only person I ever saw! Anyway you better run along and discuss this with Kashyapa. You are too young to take such a serious decision."

Jivaka ran away laughing "But I can carry you both now!"

The outcome was that Jivaka's will prevailed and both Kashyapa and Richika were embarrassed, awkward, yet very delighted and excited about the journey. Leaving Kanakhala was easy. There were mules for hire. Jivaka hired two mules and walked alongside as they started their journey. As he started describing their journey, Kashyapa was amazed at Jivaka's keen observation. Richika listened to it with such joy on his face, Kashyapa was glad that he too could be part of this joyful experience. Along the way, sometimes other pilgrims shared their food, at times they stopped in small ashrams where they were fed generously.

Jivaka kept asking people who were returning, "Are the glaciers melting? Are the mountain paths to Lanka open?"

Their first stop was Gangotri, and may be Gomukh; may be Tapovan? It all depended on how the weather held, how the glaciers behaved, how the crashing hillsides blocked the paths for days together. The mighty Himalayas and the Ganga between the two decided who was worthy of viewing them in all their splendour.

They made steady progress, starting at the crack of dawn and ending the day at three in the afternoon. Evening clouds and mist, storms and rains were hard on pilgrims. One should find safe havens by early afternoon. Night fell quickly and so completely, the warm sunny days seem like distant dream. That is when you froze to your bones.

Jivaka found both his companions bearing quite well the hardship of this long journey. Perhaps it is the beauty, perhaps it is the slow progress to higher altitudes creating a lightness in the head of an unusual kind.

Even he had felt it, as if his mind was blank and completely serene, simply resonating the mighty Himalayas. Their first sight of snow peaks came before reaching Srinagar. Jivaka stopped the mules and sent them to graze with the muleteers. He said to Richika, "This is our first view of the snow peaks, many of which are yet to come. If we reach Tapovan, we will have the closest view. Now we start with what we see at this distance—maybe twenty miles."

As they climbed up, they passed through deodar forests with lush green trees, shrubs, wild rose and jasmine. You can actually smell all these here! Richika felt the scented breeze on his face. He said excitedly, "Yes, I can smell deodar, the pine cones, the jasmines and the roses. Together they make a heady scent."

Jivaka said, "Now we take a look at a peak beyond, where this path appears to end. The trees part there, you can see a distant green mountain peak. Beyond it you see light blue peaks. Even further beyond you see standing tall, a lone snow peak! That is the Himalayan peak. It looks silvery golden on the side where the sun's rays hit, where the clouds cast a shadow, there is a metallic glint. Just looking at it sends shivers in your body. It is so cold, beautiful and formidable. I don't think I have seen anything more beautiful!"

Jivaka then fell silent to clear the clutter of the mind. Silence makes you commune with it and no one else. The three of them stood so long that the muleteers came back urging them to move ahead, take shelter in the next village before it gets dark. Kashyapa said, "Bless you, Jivaka, for bringing us here," voicing Richika's feeling too.

Jivaka said, "Masters, I am glad that I am here now in your presence. Otherwise I too would have waited like you did, and missed out something, as most people do. I am truly grateful to you both for this journey. But now onwards, there is not going to be indebtedness, from any one of us. We are here to be one with nature. Please don't ever thank me. It demeans what we experience. We are the part of the same big universe."

The three pilgrims continued their journey. Days and weeks merged seamlessly. Often in the Himalayas, you did not remember what day or week it is. Only thing that remains are days and nights. One evening, one of the muleteers said, "Now we are at Lanka. This is how far we can go! We will be picking up the returning pilgrims and going back."

Jivaka settled their dues with silver coins, collected their own meagre belongings and blankets. They were in a dense forest. The only path was the one they trod. No sign of life around. The muleteers said, "You see, below there is a ravine. You need to climb down and climb up again. It is steep but not too deep or wide. With the two old rishis you may need a couple of hours to ferry them across. Cut some sticks from these branches. It is very useful to walk up and down the inclines. Mind you, the rains make the muddy slopes rather slippery. The sticks help." The muleteers took out their hatchets and made six sticks in all for the three of them.

It was still mid-afternoon. Maybe they should aim at crossing the ravine and reach Gangotri. Kashyapa said, "I will try to walk with my sticks, you can carry Richika." The muleteers had wicker baskets for carrying the elderly. Jivaka paid more silver and bought a basket from them and settled Richika in it. While the basket rested on Jivaka's back, the ropes attached to it were strapped to Jivaka's chest.

Jivaka said laughingly, "See, it is so easy, Master, I must say you are so light that I don't even feel the weight!"

Richika murmured, "That is a relief. I would have felt bad if I were a heavy weight!" So they set off.

The ravine indeed was steep, but it was a short journey. By

early evening they were already in Gangotri. The first thing they heard was the roar of the Ganga. Richika said, "What is that thunderous sound?" Jivaka settled him, on a stone platform and Kashyapa too rested on a boulder, amazed at the spectacular form of the Ganga as she revealed herself.

Jivaka fetched water in the Kamandal, gave it to Richika and Kashyapa and had a drink himself.

"I will just take a quick dip and come back and tell you about the Ganga here in Gangotri."

After the hard trek in the heat, the glacial cold water was heavenly. Jivaka came back with his wet clothes, sat looking at the Ganga and mused aloud.

"The Ganga comes down from the glacier at Gomukh. There are gigantic boulders here, strewn all over alongside and in the middle, where the Ganga flows down. The inclines are steep and the Ganga rushes down with great force, hits the boulders, forms powerful waterfalls over and around the boulders. Each part of her path produces different sorts of waterfalls, and different musical notes, drum beats. You can actually see rainbows in the waterfalls. I will walk you around once we eat something."

There were small groups of pilgrims around and locals who come up during the pilgrimage season, vendors of food. Jivaka bought some food and they had a meal together. "Please rest on these blankets. I will find out more about what to do next" and Jivaka took off.

When he returned it was late evening, the sky had turned

red. The Ganga's roar reached a crescendo with more milling glacier water merging with it. Jivaka said, "At dusk there is an 'arati' at the Ganga temple on the top. Shall we go?" So they started. Richika in the wicker basket and Kashyapa with his two sticks.

The motley crowd of pilgrims had already gathered.

As the darkness descended, in the dim lights of the oil lamps at the door of the temple, vague forms appeared. The brass gongs and bells started, the cymbals and drums accompanied them. Richika sighed, "Such harmony resonating in the mountains. They seem to accompany the distant roar of the Ganga!"

Then the arati started. Jivaka blinked. It was the most beautiful, breathtaking sight. He had to describe it to Richika.

"You can hardly see the person holding the arati. But the flames are high and bright! The arati plate is being moved in the most unusual way.

"This one now is being moved like the dance of snake!

.... in its angry mood!

.... in its placid mood!

.... in its assured blessing!

"Now this arati is different. It flows like the Ganga.

.... calm, serene

.... angry, out of control

.... happy, joyous and bubbly

"Now this one is like a tree!

"Now this one is like lightning!

"Oh! Masters, this is unbelievable!

"Who are these miracle workers who have formed myriad ways of worshipping the Ganga!"

Then the music and arati was over as suddenly as it started. There was stunned silence.

"Oh Masters, do you know who were the creators of this magic?"

Kashyapa said, "I had heard of it but never knew it was so…indescribable. It has a quality that makes it distinct, non-Brahmanical. Possibly some tribals from Manjupattan, as it is rumoured.

"In Manjupattan, much of Hindu tradition has been adopted. Across the Himalayan range, the high shrines have visiting pilgrims from across the barrier of snow peaks to view the homes of the Hindu deities. Ganga worship is worship of nature. She is sacred to people of all castes and creeds. These terrains are hard for us from the plains. For the hill people, this was always an easy trek to the holy shrines. It is supposedly one family that carries on this tradition."

It was getting chilly. They took shelter under an overhanging rock. Jivaka collected some dry sticks and leaves, made a fire. They lay down to sleep wrapped in their blankets around the fire.

"We need to make an early start to go to Gomukh. It will take two to three days. I don't know if you want to go or we can return from here. Most people do!"

Kashyapa said, "I would like to give it a try. Oh, to go to Gomukh!"

Richika said, "I would love to go to Tapovan, where Pandavas went to die! But it depends on you, Jivaka. Do not do it if it is very hard. It is only an old man's whim!"

Jivaka said happily, "Off we are—to our early start" He turned to his side and fell asleep that instant.

Kashyapa said softly, "This is a divine child, as that washerwoman who brought him to me had said long time back!"

Richika said, "I thought you found him on the banks of the river!"

Kashyapa said, "That is what I led people to believe. I did not want any complications. He was given to my care by a washerwoman."

"But why did you accept that responsibility?"

"I will tell you one day, I am rather tired now."

"So am I," Richika said.

Next morning they trudged a distance, continuously going up hill on a bridle path. It was not a great distance, about 10 miles, but Kashyapa was already struggling as the altitude and the heat of the mid-afternoon sun were not easy on him. Jivaka carried his passenger swiftly and stopped and waited for Kashyapa to catch up. While sitting, he would describe what he saw to Richika. The pilgrims were joyous, tired and nauseous, but no one was complaining. As you climb on the winding road, far above the flowing Ganga, the tree line, nature became increasingly brutal and stark.

They halted at Bhojpas at night. They were fed by the ashramite who spent his summer there. There were many sadhus who lived throughout the year in Gangotri in the caves, despite the bitter winters. But Bhojpas and Chirbas were uninhabitable in winter when the region was blanketed in ice and snow and remained unapproachable.

Finally they were at Gomukh. The beginning of the Ganga. Jivaka said, "Tapovan plateau rests on a glacier at 15,000 feet. It is a plain in the centre of a range of mountains: Shivling is the closest one. To go there, you have to climb the crags and stretches of the glacier. Tonight we halt here. Let us see what to do next tomorrow. That is the Gomukh, out of which gushing forth is the Ganga. The front portion of this whole ice-covered glacier actually looks like the face of a cow. See, that is the ears, eyes, snout. It is a magnificent ice sculpture of a head of a cow carved out of the glacier. I wonder if it will still be there thousands of years from now!"

Kashyapa was breathless. "Unbelievable!" was all that he could say.

They watched a pilgrim taking a dip in the ice-cold water.

Kashyapa laughingly recalled Jivaka's stunt when he was only five years old, jumping into the frozen Ganga and said, "I am sure you can do it Jivaka—you did it at five!"

"But now we would like to try it in our old age. The stream is not as dangerous as in Gangotri. She is placid." Jivaka helped them with their dips.

They bought some food from a hawker where a few pilgrims were gathered. They could hardly eat. Jivaka was worried. "You must eat a little and drink lots of water. The altitude does it to you. Please rest. If you still feel sick, we will go down now."

"We will rest. We will be alright by tomorrow. This needs to get used to." The morning sun turned the Gomukh into shiny pink sculpture."

At dawn, Jivaka said, "Tapovan is only five miles away but may take me 3-4 hours. I will first take Master Richika, leave him there and come back for you. You will need more help, Master Kashyapa." He was off with Richika and the wicker basket on his back.

Holding on to crags, he climbed swiftly, using his stick to check the glacier surface before he put his foot on it. He had wrapped roughly crafted leather over his clogs. By early noon they were at Tapovan. Jivaka settled Richika on a blanket on a grass-covered mound. He said to Richika, "In front of you flows the tiny stream. When you are up to it, you can stretch your feet to touch it. In front of you is the Shivling. You can almost touch it. You have to stretch your neck a great deal to look up to it. It is shaped like a linga, another mountain looks like, it is sculpted. Please keep drinking this water." Richika was breathing hard and said nothing.

"If you are not well, I will take you down. Now we are at a great height. It is very hard to breathe."

Richika said, "No—no—I am very happy. You may go to fetch Kashyapa."

Fleet-footed Jivaka was down to fetch Kashyapa in no time. They both started climbing. It was very hard. Kashyapa could hardly breathe but did not want to give up. Jivaka held his hand and slowly pulled him up each crag. As they were approaching the peak, Kashyapa's hold slipped and his foot made a hole in the glacier surface. Jivaka sat down to examine it. Kashyapa said, "It is only a sprain, it will heal soon." Jivaka said, "Probably you are right. But right now I will carry you in the litter." They both reached to find Richika, pale, breathless and looking quite ill.

Jivaka said, "That is it! We are going down!"

Richika said, "You two go! I am staying here."

"What do you mean?"

"It was my plan all along. I want to die here, like the Pandavas did."

Jivaka was aghast. "How can you do this to me? I would not have brought you here in the first place."

Kashyapa said, "Let him have his wish."

Jivaka was angry for once. "You are a physician and your job is to give life. Not to take it away. I am a physician too. I will not take a life!"

Kashyapa calmly pacified Jivaka. "If you were his son, would you accede to his wish?"

Jivaka pondered over it.

Richika said, "I am very happy and content and in the

most beautiful place on earth. I have finished my life's work. I am totally blind and dependent and will get more and more so each day. If you were my son, I would request you to do the same. Give me a happy release."

Jivaka said, "I am not his son. I am a physician and disciple. I cannot do it to my Guru!"

Kashyapa said, "In this sacred place, I tell you the truth. Your horoscope lies in my medicine chest. Your foster mother gave it to me. Your mother was Vatsayani and your father is Richika. Her sole ambition to have a healer scholar son. I knew her. I knew her single-mindedness would make her dream come true. But I did not want to bring chaos in Richika's life. Now, as a son, would you grant him his wish?"

Jivaka turned and looked at the man who was his father. Richika called out, barely audibly, "Some water please!" Jivaka rushed and picked up the water from the sacred river and poured it into his mouth. There was a peaceful expression on his face as he lay down restfully.

Kashyapa said, "Come, let's go. It is time to go!"

Jivaka, always a physician, said, "Your ankle is still swollen" and picked up Kashyapa and sat him in the litter. Bending down, he touched Richika's feet and they started their descent.

Once down in Gomukh, Jivaka paced up and down the riverbank brooding, unlike his usual cheerful self. Kashyapa watched him mutely, feeling the sorrow of the boy as his own. After calming himself, Jivaka came and sat at Kashyapa's feet.

"Why did you not tell me? Why did you not tell Master

Richika that I was his son?"

Kashyapa stroked the bowed head of the boy.

"I had thought it over a great deal all these years. If I were to reveal the truth, it had to be told to both of you. I knew that Richika was in poor health and going progressively blind. He was himself like a child and needed to be taken care of. If I had told you the truth, what would you have done? Your mother did not want Richika to be burdened by a child. Otherwise, having loved Richika so much, she would have come back to him and faced the consequences. Richika, being an honourable man, would have married her. I knew that she wanted his son but did not want to take advantage of his goodness. Your mother wanted me to take care of you and make you a physician. The truth at times is very inconvenient, my child. I do not expect you to forgive my deception. But your mother gave me the courage of the conviction to do it this way. Otherwise, she could have sent your horoscope to Richika. She knew very well that he too lived close by. I trusted the wisdom of a mother. If you think I am wrong, I did try to make up for it by making you spend long hours serving him and learning from him. If you did not have the emotional bond with him, you would not have brought him on this pilgrimage. Neither of you were deprived of each other's affection. Perhaps I was wrong. You needed that knowledge. Please forgive me!" Kashyapa said his eyes brimming with tears.

Jivaka hugged him and said, "I was hurt and angry for being denied my father's existence. But I know that both you and my mother were right. I remember once Master Richika saying, 'He will be your eyes.' But he did not elaborate on it when I asked him to explain. Now I know that it was my mother who had said that to him. You have done exactly what she wanted you to do. Now I am not angry. Sometimes, the right action may not make you happy." Jivaka then hugged Kashyapa and wept. "I have found my father, only to lose him so soon."

Kashyapa gently soothed him, allowing him to weep.

As dusk started to fall, Jivaka stood up "My father should not die alone. I will go up and to Tapovan sit by his side, hold his hands so that he knows that his son is with him."

Next day, Jivaka came down from Tapovan by mid-afternoon. He touched Kashyapa's feet, saying, "Tata, I did the last rites of my father and came. He was so good to me, despite not knowing I was his son."

Kashyapa hugged Jivaka, stroked his face and wiped his tears and said, "I am so glad for both your parents. You are a worthy son."

The Paradise Found

Jivaka and Kashyapa were on the way on their mules to Badri—famed not only for the Badrinath temple but for the caves where Vyasamuni wrote the epic *Mahabharata* and the grand Vasundhara falls. But Jivaka and Kashyapa had another place in mind. People only heard the rumours of its existence, very few went there. There was no pilgrimage shrine there. Kashyapa said as they rested at the base of the glaciers at Govindghat, "Jivaka, I would rather go to this mysterious place: the glacier full of wonderful flowering and medicinal plants." Jivaka said, "So do I…." excitedly and went about finding out how to go there.

He came back gleefully. "Master, here at this point, we cross the river to the other side. Trek about ten miles across to that mountainside. There is not even a bridle path and we need to carry our food. Mountain springs are aplenty, we do not need to worry about water. It is not as high as Tapovan. Only as much as Gangotri and not very steep either. But looks like a dense forest. People say it is impenetrable."

They began their trek after swimming across the Alakananda river at a shallow point. After crossing, they had to crawl up to reach the other side. Above the ledge, there was no one except a saffron-robed sanyasi cooking on open fire. They went to him and greeted him. They introduced themselves as Kashyapa and Vriddajivaka.

The Baba stood up with folded hands. "I am honoured, Sirs, to be in the presence of such great physicians! What can I do for you?"

Jivaka said, "Baba, we are on the lookout for the sacred valley of flowers. People of Govindghat across Alakananda river had said, 'No one knows where it is because no one goes there.' People believe and fear they may go mad once they enter it and will never come out, as it is where the Gods inhabit. But they said Baba who lives here is a healer. He collects herbs from there and heals people!"

The Baba laughed, "I guess they also said that only a mad Baba lives there!"

Both smiled.

Baba said, "There is no trail. The valley lies in the Bhuinder pass. Alakananda river here is called Bhuinder Ganga. You go up to Gangaria village, at present it has no inhabitants. You may find an occasional brave cowherd grazing cows there the entire season. Above Gangaria there are two trails, one goes to the valley of flowers the other to Hemkund. I usually go there once a year at this time to collect the herbs and roots."

"Baba, how do you go if there is no trail?"

"I make a trail by cutting the roots and branches. I have left several stone markers."

"Please Baba, can you show us the way? We have come a long way!"

Baba said "It is my privilege to serve you. We should start now, so that we are in Gangaria by late afternoon."

He got ready quickly with a couple of hatchets, a steel pot with some burning cinders to start a fire with later and some rice and dal. He also cut three sticks to climb up with.

Jivaka asked, "What is this story about people going mad there?"

Baba said, "I believe it is a rumour started by those rishis who live around here—who do not want this most beautiful land to be violated by grazing and farming. But its beauty is indeed intoxicating. A combination of the altitude and euphoria of being there, indeed, can be considered as madness."

Trekking slowly by themselves, they reached Gangaria by evening. They found shelter below a boulder overhang. Evening brought a chill in the air as the sun went down.

Jivaka made fire with the twigs, using Baba's burning

ambers. There was a lovely little pond beckoning him. "Master, I will have a quick dip and meanwhile, I keep this pot of water for your bath." He picked up an abandoned clay pot and filled it with water. The three had a meal of dal and rice cooked on the fire in a pot they had brought.

They were up early at the usual time. Sunrise was early as they were in the middle of summer. There were two paths ahead. One to go up and another to the right. The valley of flowers nestled in the glacier in the direction of the path going to the left. Baba said, "I will leave you two to your own devices," and went in search of the herbs. "Going back is easy, on the trail that we come up," he added and bowed to them.

Jivaka said. "I am told that the flowering shrubs and trees go for miles—nearly nine miles right into the base of the mountain right on the glacier."

Kashyapa said, "What a miracle! In this inhospitable cold, wet place, a garden was created by God!"

Jivaka said. "By nature."

Kashyapa: "Alright, by nature then, until we have a proof or till God provides you with proof."

As they started up the gradual incline and winding path, the trek became very slow, not because of the difficulty of the terrain but because of the beauty of it. They both were constantly pointing out to each other the plants and flowers in great excitement.

"Look at this fern, it looks like a hooded cobra!"

"Look at this fern, it curls at the end. This plant makes

the best medicine."

"Look at the blooms on the rhododendron trees. The trees are covered with them. I can make a whole year's supply of juice out of this!"

Wherever one looked, there were flowers of all colours and fragrances. There were carpets of blue, carpets of orange and yellow! Colours as far as eyes could see: primulas, balsam, and so on. Heady fragrances of the wild roses and honey was intoxicating, indeed euphoria inducing!

"People say that people who come here get intoxicated with these heady fragrances, go into confusional states, wander off, never to be found again!"

Kashyapa nodded. "Yes, I can feel it, the heady sense of abandon: shedding off normal sense of fear or anxiety. You are right, we must not lose our sense of direction. We should take it easy. We will spend some days here, gradually getting used to this beauty, the abundance of plants, roots and flowers."

Jivaka was running around like a mountain goat while Kashyapa rested soaking in the beauty of this secret paradise!

Jivaka came back with armful of plants, roots and flowers and put them in front of Kashyapa. "Look at these! Master, have you seen anything like this?"

"Rarest of rare herbs and plants!" says Kashyapa.

By three in the noon, the clouds gathered and the winds turned chill, both returned to their shelter. They planned to spend three days there. Next day, Jivaka said, "If you don't mind, could you stay here today? I want to go to the upper path and see where it takes me. There is Hemkund there—they say."

"Yes my boy. You go and come back and tell me all about it. I will go on to the nearby trails."

"I will be back by the evening. It is three miles up and three miles down, steep though!" and went off at a brisk pace, as he was alone, on the narrow path that took him from 12,000 feet to 15,000 feet. On either side of path now were shrubs and bushes overshadowed by the dense growth of brahma kamals, pink blooms, a foot above the ground. The grey slates of the path and blushing pink of the brahma kamalas with their parrot green long stems contrasted with the light blue of the mountains and the turquoise blue sky. He said to himself, "This is unbelievable. I never thought there could exist such beauty on earth! This is the time and place, suddenly you are happy that you are alive and at the same time you are ready to die because you have seen everything you need to see on earth!"

He sat there absorbing the sheer grandeur of the place for almost two hours before heading back to the sacred paradise of flowers. Jivaka said, "Oh, look at these holy flowers of the Himalayas! 'Brahmakamala, fen kamal, kapasi and koot and Ganga tulsi'. I have never seen the likes of these before!" Kashyapa was equally thrilled.

On the third day, they ascended to the peak above the valley of flowers. There were very large rock formations surrounded by flowery meadows. The blue Himalayan poppies playing hide and seek against the grey boulders offered a contrast of strength and fragility.

As they sat there they could see the Nilgiri and Ratnavan peaks, with the grand vista of the Tipra glacier. They went ambling along the top of the glacier through the flowering meadows till they reached the river. They remembered not to wander off and headed down once again, the way they had came.

The views they saw as they came up were so different from the views they saw when they were going down. Jivaka thought, life seen through the eyes of a beautiful young man like him was like an upward journey; while going down the mountain you have a grand vista of the world as you grow old.

Jivaka exclaimed, "Tata, look at that! The splendid Himalayan mountain goat, the Thar among the glossy mountain, amongst the slippery rocks." As they were walking down a little peak, a little animal that was part-mouse and part-squirrel without a tail scampered by! Jivaka shouted "A little pika."

At the end of the day, they pored over the flowers, herbs, roots and leaves that they had collected.

Jivaka said, "Who created this paradise?"

Kashyapa said, "God!"

Jivaka said, "Nature?"

"Perhaps both!" Kashyapa added.

Journey To Manjupattan

When they returned from the dhamas, Kashyapa was totally exhausted but happy that he could fulfil his dream. Both the travellers happily settled back into the routine of being physicians. Kashyapa had sent away all the other disciples as he no longer wanted to teach. He wanted Jivaka to be free to do whatever he wanted, to be the scribe for *Kashyapa Samhita*. Jivaka got busy obtaining suitable palm leaves, the ink stains made of walnut shells. The task was as endless as was the preparation. Seeing patients was something they shared. But house calls were something Kashyapa did not do any longer. So when the servant came to say that the young mistress of the landlord nearby was rolling in pain, Jivaka went. When he reached the house, he was led to the room where the patient was. By now he had graduated to treat women's diseases.

As he stood at the doorstep, saw this astonishingly beautiful and voluptuous woman rolling on the bed, he suddenly was a man! She said, "Come Vriddha Jivaka, please treat me for this unbearable pain."She was looking at him admiringly, his physique hardened by hours of swimming.

Jivaka sighed, "This is what wisdom is all about." He recalled Kashyapa's long list of things to avoid—being with a woman alone, without an attendant was one of them.

He said politely, "Please call someone to be present, when I examine you!"

She groaned, "Oh my God—I am hurting badly—there is no one around."

"Well, then I will come back later!"

He turned away. "Oh no!" she cried.

"Don't go. There is an old woman in the kitchen, she is half blind."

Jivaka smiled, "Let her be with you, I am not blind, between the two of us we will manage."

When he returned to the ashram, he told Kashyapa what had happened at the patient's house.

Kashyapa said, "You did the right thing. It is very hard for a young man to do what you did, but for an old man like me it is easy."

"Did you have such difficulties when you were young?"

"Of course, I did, why would I warn you otherwise? Teachers are meant for that. My teacher taught me about the propriety of behaviour in a healer."

It was some years later, when *Kashyapa Samhita* was completed, a strange thing happened, disturbing the calm life that the two led. A royal emissary came from Manjupattan with a letter for Vriddha Jivaka. The man said, "I want to see Bhagwan Vriddha Jivaka. The royal physician in the court of Manjupattan has sent a letter for him." Jivaka stretched his hand, surprised to receive such a letter. "No—no—it is for Vriddha Jivaka, you must be a disciple."

Jivaka laughed. Hearing the conversation, Kashyapa came out.

The emissary turned to him and touched his feet and gave him the letter, glaring at Jivaka.

Kashyapa looked at the name and said, "Jivaka, it is for you."

The emissary said, "But he is young. How can he be Vriddha Jivaka, Sir?"

"Well, that is his title."

Jivaka read the letter aloud and said, "Master, they want me to go to Manjupattan to the royal court. But I don't want to go. Why should I go? I have enough to do here. How will you manage if I go?"

The emissary probably was someone in high position in the court. He said, "The rumours have it that Vriddha Jivaka has completed the *Kashyapa Samhita*, the only paediatric compilation in the world. The royal court has many renowned physicians—but no one is a paediatrician and qualified to deal with women's diseases."

"So?" Kashyapa asked. "Do they want to copy the book?"

"No. Sir, there is more. The king has many wives. Not one has borne him a son. Even the ones who were born died early."

Kashyapa and Jivaka looked at each other. Promiscuity among the royalty was well known all over—consequently diseases that affected the pregnancy of the wives.

"But royal physicians would know how to treat his highness."

"Sir, they personally begged that Vriddha Jivaka should be sent, so that under his guidance they can treat the king and the queens. But the main thing is that they want to learn *Kashyapa Samhita* by you and no one else."

Kashyapa said, "Give us some time to think about it!" The emissary went to the town, saying he would return the next day after visiting a relative.

Jivaka sat down looking at the compilation. "Master, I want to make illuminated calligraphy for the title. Have you done it? Will you show me?" Kashyapa took out the thin gold leaves. Some tiny gems and tree gum and showed a tiny space on a palm leaf and wrote Om!

Jivaka said, "It is so beautiful. I will sit late in the night and do the title. You will see it in the morning," very excited like a child.

"What about going to Manjupattan?"

"I don't know, you please tell me what I should do in the morning. Now I want to work on my calligraphy."

Kashyapa smiled and went to bed.

Next morning, when Jivaka woke up, Kashyapa had already gone to the banks of the Ganga.

The *Kashyapa Samhita* was open on its book holder. Jivaka remembered closing it gently after making sure the letters were dry. Curiously, he went to see the book with a lamp in his hand.

The illuminated *Kashyapa Samhita* was indeed nice. But what Jivaka saw below it was exquisitely written script, five times the size of the title, or *Vriddha Jivakiya Tantra*. Jivaka put the lamp down and ran to the banks of the Ganga. Kashyapa was in meditation. Jivaka sat at his feet and waited.

When Kashyapa opened his eyes, Jivaka cried out, "Why did you give my name—Tata? No *Samhita* has mention of the scribe's name except in passing. It is so beautiful, I cannot erase such a work of art. Why did you do it?"

Kashyapa stroked his head. "You deserve it, my child. Now, go to Manjupattan, bring fame to your Tata! Go. My blessings are with you. Take the *Samhita* with you. Let them copy it. Come back when you have completed what you have set out to do. No matter how long."

"But can you manage on your own?"

"I will ask one of the boys who trained with you to help me."

When it came to the final discussion, Kashyapa always won.

Jivaka pondered, "*Vriddha Jivakiya Tantra* indeed!"

Nama Buddha

Jivaka was amazed at the splendour of the royal court of Manjupattan. He had never seen such a palace even in Kanakhala. He was intrigued by the way Buddhism and Hinduism melded seamlessly in Manjupattan. The temples and the stupas were all venerated equally by everyone. The Chinese heritage on the architecture and faces of people made them the most beautiful to look at. He had to go back and tell Kashyapa all about this.

He was very surprised at the honour bestowed on him. He was the house guest at the house of royal physician Rajguru Sharma. The very next day of his arrival, he was taken for the audience with the King. He was draped by the King with a grand shawl and handed a silken bag of jewels and gold coins! He had never held something so valuable in his hands before.

Rajguru had fixed time for him to see all his patients separately, as they were royalty. Time passed very fast. He was also taken to every festivity in the town. In Manjupattan, nearly every day they celebrated someone or something. Mother's day, Father's day, Sister's day, Brother's day, Cow's day, the list was endless.

But the most intriguing was that of the worship of 'Kumari', the virgin young girl. The faith of the people in viewing this beautiful young girl as a reincarnation of 'devi' was amazing. He wondered how she felt in such a prison of splendour.

Meantime, Rajguru's young daughter, not so young, about seventeen years of age, played the perfect hostess to Jivaka. It was a motherless household. As Rajguru was indisposed, he did not join Jivaka for dinner that night. Saraswathi, shy as ever, with the help of servants served his meal. Suddenly Jivaka looked up at her and said, "I was at the Kumari festival today. I wondered how she felt being forced into such godly trap!"

Surprised at being addressed, she composed herself and said, "Perhaps, as I do!"

Jivaka said, "What do you mean?"

Saraswathi was silent, with downcast eyes. She said "Nothing!"

Jivaka said gently, "Tell me, I shall not tell anyone, even your father." As a physician he was obliged to say it, he thought.

But he really wanted to know why this beautiful young woman was so withdrawn and shy.

Saraswathi sighed, "My father has decided I should marry someone in Bhaktapur. The man is older, has several wives. But he is very wealthy, with a lot of property. It is rare among Brahmins to own so much wealth. As I am the only child and my father is ailing, he wants me to settle down in a wealthy household. I have seen this man. He is not bad-looking, but he is not a scholar like my father. I have heard of whispers about his being a womaniser. I spoke to my father about my reluctance. Once my father makes up his mind or gives word to someone, he would never go back on it. So I am going to be like Kumari—trapped into wealth, with nothing else!"

Jivaka said, "I don't think it is right. Why should you be forced into this marriage? You are young and beautiful. You have a long life ahead of you!"

She looked up, obviously surprised. "You think I am beautiful?"

Jivaka smiled, "Of course, there is no question about it. You are the most beautiful young woman I have ever seen!"

She blushed!

Jivaka suddenly realised that he could be mistaken for flirting with her. He said, "I am sorry. I did not mean it in any devious manner!"

She said, "I know you did not!"

The meal ended. He thanked her and went to his room.

He was restless through the night. It was most unusual for

him. He knew he was attracted to Rajguru's daughter. But it was rather woolly and vague inside his head, not verbalised or clearly thought out. Suddenly, by saying to her that she was the most beautiful woman, at that moment he had changed everything. He had taken a step he never thought he would. He needed to get away from there. Think hard and feel hard and then decide the future course of action.

In the morning, he said to Rajguru, "Sir, I need a short break. I want to go to Nama Buddha, the Buddhist shrine!"

"But you are a Hindu. Why do you want to go there?"

"I heard that the path is beautiful and the shrine is highly venerated."

"All right, I will arrange for a horse and a guide."

"Thank you, sir, but no. I want to walk all the way. I find walking a meditative experience."

"All right, take care. You are a young, strong man. You should make it easily."

Walking was indeed meditative. The beauty of the meadows, the forest paths, the gliding streams seemed endless. On the third day, he climbed the hill that led to the Buddhist shrine. He rang the brass bells all the way up to the shrine. He had expected a grand shrine. He found a small shrine with a carved stone tablet. He was amazed. It depicted the story of Buddha in a crude carving of figures of the Buddha, a tigress with two cubs. The story was that at this spot, a starving mother tiger came with her two young cubs. She saw the Buddha in meditation. She begged the Buddha to give her and her cubs some flesh—otherwise they would die. The ever-benevolent Buddha, not having anything to give to the mother tiger, cut his own flesh and fed her.

Jivaka had tears in his eyes. How petty and selfish we human beings are. When you have compassion, pain of others becomes your own pain. You sacrifice your self to relieve that pain.

Jivaka returned to the Yambu valley with a light heart. *Vriddha Jivakiya Tantra* was of no significance. It was only a book. His return was greeted with cheer by Rajguru and his daughter. Rajguru neither saw her sad face before, nor the joyous one this night. After dinner, Jivaka sought Rajguru's audience.

"Sir, I happen to discover that your daughter is unhappy about the betrothal you have arranged. Is it possible for you to revoke it?"

Rajguru was aghast at the young man's audacity. He spluttered, "How dare you question my decision about my own daughter?"

Sarcastically he added "Whom do you suggest in your infinite wisdom, I should marry her off to instead?"

Jivaka looked up and said, "Me—perhaps."

"You, a pauper Brahmin from Kanakhala, remember who you are talking to. There is nothing more to be said. You may leave!" *The Vriddha Jivakiya Tantra* was with Rajguru under lock and key.

As Jivaka came out, Saraswathi came, touched his feet and said, "Thank you. You have tried your best. I told you I am imprisoned like Kumari. There is no way out."

Jivaka said, "I meant it when I said I will marry you—because I love you. But your father is right. I am a pauper. All I have is what the king has given me."

Saraswathi said softly, "I love you too. I have, ever since I set eyes on you, the day you arrived here with your book."

Jivaka said, "There is nothing to prevent us from getting married. If you are happy to accompany me to Kanakhala and lead a simple life, I can marry you at this moment."

Saraswathi's face shimmered with tears of joy!

She said, "Jivaka, I will follow you to the end of the world. But when and how do we get married?"

Jivaka said, "Let us go to te ɿple of Narayani and wait and get married as soon as the priest arrives at dawn."

Saraswathi said, "But your book—it is with my father. The moment you ask for it, he will suspect that you are up to something."

Jivaka said, "Saraswathi—here the choice is between the most beautiful woman whom I have come to love and the book I scribed. I can write it again. But I cannot let you go!"

They left with the clothes they had on, the purse containing the King's gift and started towards the Narayani shrine.

In the early hours of dawn, a young man and a young woman waited near the temple. Jivaka admired the reclining Vishnu on seven-hooded Sesha. The Vishnu and Sesha sculpture almost filled the water tank. It was unbelievably enormous and Vishnu's face was full of compassion. The local lore was that royalty should never visit this particular shrine.

A priest came to start the puja of the day. Jivaka and Saraswathi touched his feet. Jivaka said, "I am from Kanakhala. I have no parents. I want to marry this girl and take her home as my bride."

The priest asked him, "Will you provide for her and cherish her as your partner?"

"Yes, I am a physician of children. I can support us." The priest performed the ceremony simply, according to the Hindu rites. Jivaka gave one gold coin to the priest and sought his blessings for a long journey and happy married life.

The Present

In Manjupattan, 1938

Years and years later, in 1938, Rajguru Hemaraja Sharma of the Royal Court of Manjupattan, now known as Nepal, was astounded and excited to discover the treatise, *Kashyapa Samhita* or *Vriddha Jivakiya Tantra*. Upon studying it, he decided that it definitely deserved the second name. He wondered how this tome came to be among the heirlooms of one of the earlier Rajgurus, centuries before.

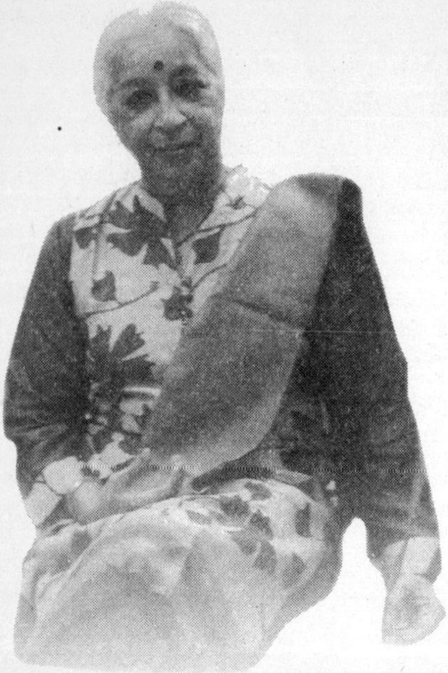

Malavika Kapur is a clinical psychologist working with children. She is a visiting professor at the National Institute of Advanced Studies. She was the Professor and Head of the Department of Clinical Psychology at the National Institute of Mental Health and Neurosciences, Bangalore. As a professional she has several books and national and international publications to her credit.

The mysteries of the human mind have always fascinated Malvika and she has deep interest in ancient India's approach to childcare. Writing fiction offers her a perfect blend of psychology and creative fantasy. She has two anthologies to her credit, *The Lost Soul and Other Stories* and *Ghosts and Other Friends*. Her adventure story for children, *Adventures at Kudremukh* was published in 2004. One of her stories, 'Nessy of Lochness', for children has been awarded a prize by the Children's Book Trust in 2002.

Daughter of renowned Kannada writer and Jnanapeeta award winner **Shivarama Karanth**, Malavika is a prolific reader with deep interest in the performing arts. She is an inveterate traveler and loves trekking in the Himalayan foothills.